The MAGICIAN'S APPRENTICE

The MAGICIAN'S APPRENTICE

Tom McGowen

LODESTAR BOOKS E. P. Dutton New York

No character in this book is intended to represent any actual person; all the incidents of the story are entirely fictional in nature.

Library of Congress Cataloging in Publication Data

McGowen, Tom.
The magician's apprentice.

"Lodestar books."
Summary: A young pickpocket becomes apprenticed to a magician who opens a whole new world for the boy, not only of magic and healing, but of kindness and adventure. Together they seek knowledge lost since the Age of Magic, thousands of years before.
[1. Fantasy] I. Title.
PZ7.M47849Mag 1987 [Fic] 86-19743
ISBN 0-525-67189-7

Published in the United States by E.P. Dutton, a division of Penguin Books USA Inc.

Published simultaneously in Canada by Fitzhenry & Whiteside Limited, Toronto

Editor: Rosemary Brosnan Designer: Annie Alleman

Printed in the U.S.A. W
10 9 8 7 6 5 4

for Grant and Nicky

• • • 1 • • •

A frightened man was hurrying down a dark, silent street in a night-shrouded city. He cast quick, apprehensive glances in all directions as he went, and kept his hand on the hilt of a knife that hung in a sheath at his hip. His clothing marked him as a well-to-do member of the merchant class, and he was mentally cursing the folly that had kept him carousing in a tavern until darkness had closed over the city. For while by day the city's streets were thronged with busy, surging crowds, sundown saw them turn into black, winding ribbons that were shunned by honest folk and prowled by members of the city's underworld—beggars, pickpockets, gangs of youths who took pleasure in beating senseless any lone traveler they encountered, and ruthless men and women who would cut a man's throat for a single iron coin. Praying he would not meet any of these creatures of darkness, the merchant gripped his stone-bladed knife and trotted nervously on his way.

Ahead of him glowed a welcome patch of light cast

by a small lantern above the door of a house. Gratefully, the man headed for it, but as he entered the rim of the dim illumination a small ragged figure materialized out of the darkness beyond and darted at him. The merchant gave a squawk of dismay and jerked the knife from its sheath. But a high-pitched voice was whining: "Good man, kind man, please spare a coin, just a bit of iron, for a poor hungry orphan," and the hands that clutched at him reached no higher than his chest. A child.

The merchant jerked his arm away from the softly clutching fingers. "Get away," he said hoarsely, and gave the urchin a shove that sent him sprawling to the ground.

The beggar lay face down in the dim yellow pool of light and sent up a soft, thin wailing. The merchant, his heart pounding from the terror that had momentarily gripped him, broke into a run and vanished from sight in the darkness.

When the man's footfalls had died away in the distance, the boy abruptly ceased his sobbing. He rolled nimbly up to a cross-legged position, and with a quick jerk of his head tossed back the tangle of black hair that had fallen over his eyes. His teeth flashed in a mocking grin as he examined the contents of the money bag he had slipped from the merchant's tunic even as the man had been pushing him away.

The boy sorted out the coins and hissed with pleasure. A dozen irons, four coppers, and a silver! Old Paplo, who had taught him the art of picking pockets, had given him a quota of two irons a day to bring home. If the boy turned in that sum, or more, Paplo fed him and permitted him to sleep in a corner of the tiny hovel that was the old man's dwelling. Less than that, and the boy was cursed, slapped, and turned away to find his food and shelter as best he could. So the contents of this money bag, doled out a little at a time, would keep old Paplo placated, and the boy fed and housed, for a good many days.

Of course, he'd not turn everything over to the old man. He would take the silver piece to a money changer who'd give him at least seven coppers for it, and those he would use for fun—a visit to the Street of Sweetmakers, a seat at a dogfight, and a goodly quantity of skewers of spiced roasted meats and other delicacies he seldom had an opportunity to enjoy.

Hopping lithely to his feet, the boy stuffed the money bag into his ragged smock and prepared to saunter on his way. He had taken no more than a step when a loud cough made him glance toward the doorway over which hung the lantern that spread its little glow upon this patch of street. A man had just emerged from the house and was standing with one hand on the door's handle. He was a tall, fat man, wearing the ankle-length gown of pale blue that marked him as a sage—an astrologer, dream explainer, or some similar occupation that dealt with the realms of knowledge and wisdom. The lantern light showed him to have a youthfully smooth face that seemed at odds with the ring of pure white hair that formed a fringe around a shining bald head. The man directed a brief, incurious glance at the ragged figure of the little boy, then coughed again, noisily, bending over with a fist to his mouth. Then he straightened, unhooked the lantern, and with it swinging in his hand moved off down the street. Being a sage, he, of course, had no fear of the dark and dangerous streets; robbers and brigands left such men alone lest powerful curses be placed on them.

The boy's eyes followed the glimmer of swaying light until it melted into darkness, then he flicked his glance back to the entrance of the house. It seemed to him that the man had left the door ajar without noticing it, and after a moment this was confirmed when the boy became aware of a dim line of light coming from inside the house, marking the narrow opening.

The boy quickly moved to the door. Gently, he pushed it open a bit more and poked his head through the doorway. A thin candle was burning in a wall niche near the door, probably left there by the sage so that he wouldn't have to fumble about in darkness when he returned, but the rest of the house was pitch-black and silent. There did not seem to be anyone within.

The boy licked his lips and pondered for a moment. To enter the home of a sage for the purpose of robbery was to take a dreadful chance. The house might well be protected by a spell that would bring swift death to a burglar. On the other hand, the thought of the treasures he might find acted as a spur to the boy. With a silent prayer to Durbis, the spirit who watches over thieves, he slipped past the door and closed it behind him.

Digging into the twisted length of cloth that served him both as sash and pocket, he withdrew a stump of candle and lit it from the candle burning in the niche. Holding the light at arm's length, he moved cautiously into the depths of the house.

There were only a few rooms, and he examined them all, peering into every corner. He found nothing of any real value: some clothing in a chest in a room with a sleeping mat; writing materials on a shelf in a room with painted walls; and clay cups, dishes, and cooking pots in a room with an open fireplace. From this room he followed the light into a short hall at the end of which was a door. Pulling open the door, he beheld a flight of irregular stone steps, winding down into darkness.

"Perhaps he keeps his valuables and magical things hidden in the cellar," muttered the boy. His bare feet moved noiselessly on the stairs. The door softly bumped shut behind him.

The steps led down into a single room dug out of the earth and walled with stones and mortar. As the boy moved cautiously forward, the candle revealed a broad wooden table cluttered with clay bottles and beakers and a variety of objects that were totally unfamiliar to him. He looked them over for a moment, then, seeing nothing worth taking, moved toward a large cabinet that stood in one corner.

At that moment there was a faint squeak from the top of the stairs. The door, which the boy knew had closed behind him, had been opened by someone.

Terror flooded the boy, but he did not lose his wits. In an instant he had blown out the candle and wiggled his way as far as he could go beneath the table. Perhaps whoever was coming down the stairs would not see him and he could make his escape later. Heart pounding, he waited.

Heavy footsteps padded down the stairs. A figure, holding the lantern that had hung over the house's doorway, moved ponderously into the cellar. It paused, and the glow of light danced on the walls as the lantern was lifted and moved about. Then the figure came to the table, stooped down, and spilled light upon the small ragged figure crouched there. Sick with fear, the boy stared back into the face that was revealed by the lantern light—a smooth, fleshy face with a fringe of white hair surrounding a bald head. It was the sage.

The man gazed solemnly at the shivering boy. "Now," he said in a deep pleasant voice, "if I were a spider and you were a fly, you'd be in serious trouble—eh?"

◆ ◆ ◆ 2 ◆ ◆ ◆

The boy's fear dissolved into astonishment. He had expected a bellow of surprise and a rain of blows and kicks, but it was obvious that the man had expected to find him here. The boy considered that. It could only mean that he had been deliberately trapped. The loud coughs had been to attract his attention, the door had been left ajar to entice him—the man had obviously wanted him to enter the house, had given him time to do so, and then had come back to catch him. Why?

The man hooked one foot around the leg of a nearby stool and pulled it to him. With a grunt, he seated himself, the lantern dangling from his hand. "You may come out from under there now," he suggested amiably.

The boy eased his way from beneath the table and warily stood up. His eyes darted about. The man had placed himself in such a way that he blocked the stairs, so escape was out of the question at the moment.

The boy studied his captor. Like the boy himself and most of the other inhabitants of the city, the man was dark-eyed and tan-skinned. His features were fine and regular; he had probably been handsome as a young man. A single earring, a tiny ball of polished blue stone, dangled from a delicate chain in his left ear. Although at first glance he seemed fat and slow-moving, the boy had the feeling that he would be able to move with catlike quickness if he chose and that his bulk was more muscular than flabby. There was an air of calm authority about him, as if he would make himself master of most any situation. And, the boy reflected sourly, he was certainly master of this one.

The man was also studying the boy. His first impression was of a barefoot, undernourished child in soiled leg wrappings and a ragged smock that was far too big. The boy resembled any of the other ill-fed, unclean, uneducated urchins that swarmed in the gutters of Ingarron city. But there were subtle differences. He did not slouch; he held himself erect, with poise. And the dark eyes in the thin face framed by the mop of black hair were alert and intelligent.

"My name," said the man after a time, "is Armindor. Armindor the Magician."

The boy darted him a worried glance but made no reply. Armindor waited for a bit, then said, "And what is your name?

"Tigg."

"How old are you, Tigg?"

The boy shrugged. "About twelve summers. Maybe half a summer older or younger."

"Have your parents never told you your exact age?" asked the man.

"I have no parents."

"An aunt or uncle? Older sister or brother? Anyone?"

Again the boy shrugged. "There's an old man called Paplo, but I'm not related to him—I don't think. I steal for him so he can get drunk. He gives me food and lets me sleep in his house if I steal enough to satisfy him."

"I see. Then you have no family." said Armindor. It seemed to Tigg that the man was pleased about that.

"What are you going to do to me?" demanded the boy. He knew that he was completely in this man's power and had no illusions as to what that might mean. Armindor could beat him senseless, abuse him in any way he chose, or even kill him. He could sell Tigg into slavery, or turn him over to the city judges, who would have his thumbs cut off so that he could never pick pockets again. But somehow, Tigg felt that the man did not intend any of those things.

"Well, now," said Armindor, in answer to Tigg's question, "I certainly think you must be punished in some way for trying to rob me. Justice demands it. Don't you agree?"

Tigg eyed him. The man's tone was deliberately bantering, and the boy wondered why. He had seen enough of human nature in his young life to be able to sense the intention of malice and cruelty, and he did not sense these things in Armindor's manner. He felt that the man was probing, looking for some special kind of reaction, and Tigg believed this must have something to do with the reason why he had been trapped. He decided to match the magician's bantering manner and see what happened.

He assumed what he knew to be an expression of injured innocence—it had gotten him out of more than one predicament before this. "But, Great Magician, I *didn't* rob you," he pointed out. "You can see for yourself that none of your things are missing. How can you punish me for something that wasn't done? *That* wouldn't be justice, now would it?"

The magician's lips twitched and Tigg inwardly rejoiced; he had apparently chosen the right course. "There is some truth in what you say," said Armindor, nodding. "Very well then, we shall make the punishment fit the situation exactly. You planned to take something from me, but I still have everything that is mine, as you remarked. So, as a punishment I shall take something that is yours—and yet, you too will keep everything you have."

The boy puzzled over this for a moment, trying to fathom Armindor's meaning. "I don't understand," he said.

Armindor leaned forward, causing the stool to creak. "I'll explain. You have three valuable possessions—poise, courage, and wit. I saw the poise when I watched you so neatly relieve that merchant of his money bag. That was when I decided to—invite you into my home. I saw the courage when you didn't break into shrieks and tears when I discovered you under the table. And I saw the wit when you answered my last question. Well, I have been looking for a young person with just those qualities. You see, I have decided that I need an apprentice. And now I have found one—you." He smiled. "Thus your punishment will be effected. As my apprentice you will give me the use of your poise, courage, and wit, while of course continuing to keep them yourself."

Tigg, who had been smirking with pleasure at the magician's praise of his qualities, was suddenly plunged into an abyss of shock. Apprentice? Apprentice to a magician? But that would mean the end of his freedom, the end of his whole way of life! It would mean, he felt sure, work: long hours of work—and probably of *study* as well!

Subduing the grimace he felt like making, he slid a charming smile onto his face. "Why, that would be an honor, Great Magician! What a wonderful bit of luck for me! I always wanted to be a magician's apprentice!" I'll pretend to bow to the old fool's wishes, he thought, and as soon as he's looking the other way I'll skip away from here and never come within a thousand steps of the Street of Sages again!

But Armindor was regarding him with twinkling eyes and the faintest suspicion of a smile twitching at his mouth. The man placed the lantern on the table, then stood up and gently but firmly took hold of Tigg's arm. With the boy in his grip, he moved to the large wooden cabinet that stood against the wall in a corner and opened its doors. He took something from a shelf, nudged the doors shut, and guided Tigg back to the table, where he put down the thing he had taken from the cabinet. Tigg saw that it was a small wax figure, shaped like a human, with arms, legs, and a head.

From the loose sleeve of his gown, Armindor drew forth a small sharp-edged dagger. Before Tigg knew what was happening, the man had grasped a lock of his hair, sawed it off with a quick movement of the knife, and dropped it onto the table beside the wax figure.

"Give me your hand," he commanded.

Tigg did so without thinking, then yelped as the dagger pricked his thumb, drawing forth a bright drop of blood. Armindor picked up the doll and pressed the boy's thumb against it, smearing it with blood. Then he pushed the clump of Tigg's hair into the round lump that served as the doll's head, working the wax with his fingertips until the hair was firmly stuck in place.

"Now," he said, holding the doll under Tigg's nose,

"this is *you*! I have your spirit in this simulacrum, Tigg, no matter where you may be. Whatever I do to this will happen to you! If I cut off its arm, *your* arm will shrivel and fall off! If I drop it into a fire, *your* body will burn and melt as the simulacrum burns and melts!"

Tigg stared in terror at the lumpy figure. He knew full well the power that magicians had over people whose simulacrums they possessed. He shivered.

"All right, then," said Armindor softly, smiling and putting the doll gently on the table. "As long as I have this, I'll know that you'll be glad to stay with me and become my apprentice. You wouldn't dream of trying to run away, would you—apprentice?"

Tigg sighed. "No, Great Magician," he agreed. "Just tell me what I have to do."

· · · 3 · · ·

Tigg took up his abode with Armindor at once. The man showed him to a small room in which there was a thick sleeping mat and bade him good dreams. The boy had never slept on anything but the dirt floor of old Paplo's hovel or the rubbish-strewn bit of riverbank beneath a bridge that provided a roof against the rain, so the mat was a delightful luxury. He stretched out on it, began to ponder his sudden change of fortune, and promptly fell asleep.

He was awakened by Armindor far too early the next morning and arose prepared to be sullen and resentful at his captivity. His sullenness could not hold up against the sight of a breakfast of fried bread and vegetable paste, which Armindor assured him was for him. Breakfast was also a little-known luxury for Tigg; old Paplo had never provided it, and Tigg had usually gone without unless he was able to steal something from a vendor's stall. He was astounded to realize that Armindor intended to give him a breakfast every day, and a small portion of his resentment broke off and went drifting away.

However, it quickly became apparent that, as he had foreseen, a magician's apprentice, like any other kind of apprentice, had to devote most of his waking hours to work and study. But the boy was quite surprised to find this far less unpleasant than he had feared. The work was minimal; it amounted only to keeping the house and cellar moderately tidy, running errands, helping Armindor prepare magical materials, and watching as Armindor dealt with the numerous customers who came to him for magical services. As for the study, to Tigg's amazement, that actually turned out to be sheer pleasure!

At first he was appalled when Armindor informed him that a magician's apprentice must know how to read and work with numbers. Tigg had never been to school, of course, for there were no schools for ordinary children of the city—much less beggars, thieves, and pickpockets—nor had any of the adults he'd known been capable of reading or doing arithmetic. Those were things done only by priests, sages such as Armindor, and merchant's secretaries. Tigg had never even considered trying to learn to read and write, and it seemed an absolute impossibility. "I can't do it!" he protested.

"Yes, you can," Armindor told him gently. He showed Tigg a flat, thin square of wood upon which a number of painted characters were arranged in rows. "Now, this is called an alphabet. . . . "

When, after a time, Tigg grasped that each mark in the row of marks stood for a sound and that these sound marks could be fitted together to make words, he felt as if a door to a delightful garden had been thrown open and he had been invited to come play in it. There was a longing in him, it seemed, which he hadn't even known about until now, to learn and discover new things.

"Now you are truly on the way to becoming a magician," Armindor told him, "for knowing how to read and write, and do a few other things I shall show you, is the basis of magic." From a pocket within his robe he drew forth a number of sheets of smooth, whitish cloth, all sewn together at one edge and covered with painted words. "This is a book of spells, and every spell in it is one I copied down from some other source. You see, most spells were discovered long, long ago and were preserved by many generations of magicians who carefully copied them down. That is why it is essential for a magician to be able to read and write."

After a few days Armindor introduced Tigg to the other things he had hinted at—the manipulation of numbers. The boy found this, too, to be a source of delight. He knew how to count, up to ten anyway, but he had never dreamed that numbers could be taken apart, put together in different ways, and balanced and juggled as Armindor showed him, using wooden disks. It was like a fascinating game.

There was also the surprising bonus that Armindor never once struck him. Tigg had been prepared for beatings such as he had often received from old Paplo and other adults of his acquaintance, but they never came. Unlike the swarming, poverty-ridden, hovel-dwelling people Tigg had lived among until now, who seemed to spend their lives in a steady grip of rage that frequently flared into curses, blows, and violence, Armindor never lost his temper, never raised his voice. If Tigg made an error at his lessons, the man calmly pointed it out; if the results of Tigg's cleaning tasks were less than satisfactory, Armindor merely suggested that he do them over. Without even being aware of it, Tigg soon slipped into an effort to do his best to please the magician. While he would have resented beatings and scoldings, it became a matter of pride to do things so well that Armindor would never have to mention any shortcomings.

Armindor's magical services seemed to be in great demand; several times each day Tigg watched and listened as the man dealt with someone who sought his help. Many of those who came to him had one of the many sicknesses or maladies that were common throughout the city, and for them Armindor dispensed various potions, pills, and powders with meticulous instructions. "This spell has a sharp and stinging taste the boy will not like," he might tell the mother of a child with a wheezing chest and racking cough, "but you must make him swallow half an eggshellful at dawn, midday, and dusk, to open his throat so that he may breathe properly." At the back of Armindor's dwelling was a small garden in which the magician grew herbs and flowers that were used in making these healing spells, and Tigg learned it would be one of his duties to become familiar with all the plants and their uses.

Other people came to Armindor mainly for knowledge of what their future might hold. For them the magician asked many questions, studied the pattern formed by a number of small, oddly carved bits of bone that he would cast into a bowl, and consulted the complicated charts and diagrams painted on the walls of the room in which he met with his clients. He would then tell the person what to expect and offer advice for countering bad fortune and increasing good. This art, too, Tigg was to learn.

So the boy's days were full and not at all unpleasant. But nevertheless, Tigg chafed at the feeling that he was not free. He had, after all, been forced into this situation. He was being made to start all over and learn a new profession when he already had a perfectly good profession at which he was highly skilled. He was proud of his ability as a pickpocket and not at all sure that he wanted to become a magician instead. He was often seized with a yearning to go out once more into a crowd of people and pit his clever fingers against the unnoticing stupidity of the thronging grown-ups. He sometimes pondered the idea of breaking into the cabinet in Armindor's cellar, stealing the wax image, and carrying it off with him so the magician wouldn't be able to use it to punish him. Then he would find himself thinking of his comfortable sleeping mat, his regular meals, the rather interesting things he was doing, and the kindness with which Armindor treated him, and he would feel ashamed. The fact was, he didn't know whether to regard Armindor as a kindly rescuer or as a slavemaster.

Nor did he quite know how to regard Armindor's work. Although the man did have a thriving business and plenty of clients, Tigg noticed that he charged most of them, especially those who seemed needy, only nominal sums for his services, and so he seemed to make hardly enough money to get by. Yet he appeared to be almost wealthy. Armindor also had frequent meetings with other blue-robed sages, all of whom, the sharp-eyed Tigg had noticed, wore little blue earrings like the one in Armindor's ear. These men seemed to treat Armindor with considerable respect, and it occurred to Tigg that the man might be something more than just an ordinary magician. The boy sensed a mystery.

When he had been with Armindor for nearly a moon, there was a sudden surprise. He finished breakfast one morning and looked up to see the magician watching him thoughtfully.

"You are doing very well, Tigg. Better than I had even hoped for," the man told him. "I see no reason to wait any longer to carry out the plan I needed you to help me with. In two days a merchant caravan will be leaving on a trip to the city of Orrello on the Silver Sea. You and I will make that trip with the caravan." He stood up. "I must go and make some purchases. While I am gone, you can pack the things we shall need to take to Orrello with us. You'll find them, together with some bags, piled in a corner of the room where I usually meet with clients." Then he strode out of the room, and after a moment Tigg heard the front door close.

The boy's thoughts raced. He knew that Orrello was some twenty days' journey to the north, through uninhabited country. Once he set out on such a journey he was committed to staying with Armindor until the man returned home to this city of Ingarron. Tigg realized this was his chance, and he had to take it *now,* while he could still escape into the streets of Ingarron.

He sprang to his feet, snatched up the burning candle that sat on a shelf nearby, and sped to the cellar. He remembered that the lock on the cabinet in the cellar was a heavy contrivance of intermeshing wooden pegs that was opened with an intricately carved wooden key, but he felt that if he couldn't coax it open somehow he would simply break it or chop it. Down in the cellar he made his way around the littered table and held the candle toward the cabinet door.

The lock was gone. The door was slightly ajar.

Tigg stood motionless with surprise for several seconds. Then he reached out and nudged the door fully open. The candle glow revealed his simulacrum, lying all by itself on the center shelf. All he had to do was pick it up, run upstairs, and dart out the front door, and he would be free again. He could even, if he wished, take a few moments to help himself to some of Armindor's belongings, which would probably fetch a good price in the thieves' market of Ingarron.

But the boy stared at the little waxen figure and gnawed his lip. It was obvious that Armindor had set another trap for him, only this wasn't a trap to ensnare him as the first one had been, it was a trap to force him to make a choice. Armindor was showing him that he could leave if he wished, without any fear of punishment. The man was even offering the thief the chance to rob him, if that was Tigg's wish.

Tigg pondered. Why was Armindor doing this? The boy turned the question over in his mind.

He's left it up to me to decide whether to go or stay, thought Tigg. He's showing me that I really am free. But—he must *want* me to stay, or else he'd have just given me the simulacrum and told me to go. And he's trusting me not to rob him.

He wants me to stay with him. He trusts me.

No one had ever trusted him before. He had never been shown that anyone wanted him before. With strange feelings that he didn't quite understand, Tigg carefully closed the cabinet and hurried upstairs to begin packing.

♦ ♦ ♦ 4 ♦ ♦ ♦

Tigg shifted his weight and groaned.

Pod, the gangling, teenage youth who was driving the cart in which Tigg rode, glanced at him with a grin. "What's the matter, young one? Bottom gone to sleep?"

That was precisely what *was* the matter, but Tigg merely scowled and remained silent. When the caravan had started out yesterday morning, he had been quite excited at the prospect of the journey, for he had never been outside Ingarron in all his twelve years. But hours and hours of sitting on a dreadfully hard wooden plank in a cart that bounced and bumped over the rough trail had dulled his enthusiasm—and his posterior. He seemed able to sit in one position only for a short time before the part of his body in contact with the plank began to lose feeling. Then he would have to squirm and wiggle to bring the blood back into his legs and rump. This was a source of amusement to Pod, the apprentice merchant cart-driver, who, from the lofty vantage of several years' seniority, was continually addressing Tigg as young one—a title which Tigg found most infuriating.

The caravan consisted of eight huge wooden carts pulled by teams of the giant piglike creatures known as squnts. The carts, painted in the orange and maroon of the Pynjo Merchandising Company, were loaded with trade goods and were driven by apprentice merchants, some of about Tigg's age but most slightly older. Pynjo, the master merchant, rode at the head of the caravan on a costly golden orange horse and was accompanied by half a dozen senior merchants, merchants, and secretaries mounted on hornbeasts. There was also a small number of travelers riding in the wagons who had paid to journey with the caravan to avail themselves of the protection of the troop of soldiers that was on hand to guard Pynjo's property. There were two dozen of these soldiers: hard-faced men and women in knee-length leather coats covered with overlapping scales of horn, and armed with crossbows and quivers of stone-tipped arrows, stone-headed battle maces, and long lances. They were necessary, these soldiers, for much of the countryside between cities was a howling wilderness filled with dangers. Caravans were often attacked by bands of brigands, and there were many large, dangerous beasts that sometimes carried off hornbeasts, people, and even squnts. When the caravan halted at sunset, the wagons were drawn into a circle, fires were kept burning through the night, and groups of soldiers took turns standing guard.

Tigg shifted his weight again, and for the umpteenth time wondered if he shouldn't have, after all, taken the simulacrum and run away back in Ingarron. He hadn't anticipated all this boredom and discomfort. The morning dragged on with the same monotony as the unchanging countryside. Finally, when the sun was straight overhead, a horn sounded from the front of the caravan, signaling the midday halt. The wagons creaked to a stop, and the apprentices hopped down to stretch their legs.

Tigg, too, clambered from his seat to the ground and began to stamp his feet to bring circulation back into his legs. A sudden distant shout made him turn his head. One of the soldiers, riding in toward the wagons, had brought his mount to a halt and was peering down at something on the ground.

"Hoh, Commander Yomer," the man called to his leader, "there's a grubber lying here. Seems to be hurt."

This was interesting news to Tigg. Grubbers were furry little cat-size creatures that walked on two legs and lived in underground tunnels they rapidly dug with their large, handlike, claw-tipped paws that formed excellent shovels. It was said they could make fire and that they had a language and were sometimes even able to learn the tongue of humans if taught to do so. Tigg had seen one once—a caged captive of a traveling circus. He remembered it as a pitiful, bedraggled creature begging for food in a squeaky, oddly accented voice. Eager to see one of the little beasts at close range, he sprinted out to where the soldier had halted.

Commander Yomer, the leader of the soldiers, had ridden to join the soldier too. Beside the front hoofs of his horse lay a small furry shape. It stirred feebly as Tigg arrived and stared up at him with bright, black, pain-filled eyes in a bearlike face.

Commander Yomer leaned out of his saddle, peering down. "It has been clawed by some other beast," he observed. "The poor thing is as good as dead. Put it out of its pain, Timas." He tugged his horse around and trotted off. Timas, the soldier who had found the creature, unslung his lance and drew back his arm, aiming with care. The grubber gave a shuddering sigh and closed its eyes.

"No!" Tigg heard himself yell. He thrust his body in the path of the lance, straddling the wounded creature. "Don't kill him! I—I'll try to help him."

The man pursed his lips and shook his head. "He's past help, boy. Believe me, I've seen many a wound, and he's got a bad one. Like the commander says, he's half dead."

Tigg knelt beside the small form. "I don't care. I'm going to try to save him." He was a little surprised at the compassion he felt for the grubber; Durbis knows there had been little enough compassion shown *him* during his twelve years. But he was determined to do what he could for the creature.

"Well, suit yourself." The soldier slipped the lance thong back over his shoulder. "But don't take it hard when he dies." He clicked his mount into a trot and headed for the carts.

Tigg stared down at the grubber. A long puckered gash crossed the width of its chest, and its grayish fur was sticky with half-dried blood. Well, perhaps the first thing to do would be to bathe the wound. That meant getting the creature back to the wagons, where there were water bags.

As gently as he could, Tigg worked his arms beneath the grubber's body. It made a faint whimpering sound, but he felt that it knew he was trying to help it. He rose slowly, and with the grubber cradled in his arms walked carefully back to the caravan.

Armindor, arms folded over his chest and a peculiar expression on his face, watched as the boy approached the carts. "Now, what do you propose to do with this poor half-dead thing?" he asked as Tigg drew abreast of him.

"I want to help it."

"Why? So you can put it in a cage and charge people to look at it? Or do you plan to teach it how to steal money bags for you?"

"No!" Tigg exclaimed angrily. "I just want to help it!"

Armindor continued to look at him for a few moments, then took a step forward and bent over the grubber, peering at the bloody wound on its body. He straightened up and turned away. "It needs more help than you can give it," he said over his shoulder. "Come."

Tigg followed the magician to the side of the wagon in which Armindor was making the journey. A shelf running along the length of the side bore bundles and boxes that contained travelers' belongings, and Armindor removed a large, bulging bag from among the others. Placing this on the ground, he rummaged within it and brought forth a large rectangular chest.

With loud grunts and explosions of breath, he eased himself to the ground, crossed his legs, and opened the chest. It was actually a box with a single drawer that pulled onto his lap, leaving the flat top of the box as a work surface. Onto this the magician placed a thick, square candle, taken from the drawer. With a flint-and-metal sparkmaker and a tinderbox, he kindled a tiny blaze and applied it to the candlewick. The blue spiral of smoke that arose had a strong, sweetish odor.

Next Armindor withdrew several stoppered clay bottles, a wide-mouthed clay pot, and a thick roll of white cloth. He poured a small quantity of the substance in each bottle into the pot—a pinch of greenish powder, five drops of an oily amber liquid, half a pinch of white powder. A brownish rod of what appeared to be carved bone was held for a moment in the candle flame, then used to briskly stir the contents of the pot.

"Kneel down here so I can reach the creature," the magician commanded. Tigg quickly complied, and with the tip of the bone rod Armindor gently covered the grubber's wound with a thick, strong-smelling paste that had formed in the pot. Then, several lengths of the roll of white cloth were wound around the grubber's chest and knotted securely.

"All right," said Armindor. He blew out the candle. "That is a very good healing spell; I think your furry friend will survive." He began stuffing the bottles, candle, and pot back into the drawer.

Standing over the magician with the now slumbering grubber cradled in his arms, Tigg felt he should say something. He was aware that it was mainly for him that Armindor had used his magical skill and knowledge to save the little creature's life. He cleared his throat. "Uh—thank you, Armindor."

The magician was wiping the bone rod on the grass. His eyes flicked upward and met Tigg's. "You can't be carrying the creature around like that forever. Wait just a moment and I'll show you how to make a bed for it in your wagon."

· · · 5 · · ·

"Big city," said Tigg.

"Bick city," said the grubber.

"It sure is something," remarked Pod, "how you've taught him to talk!"

Twenty days had passed since Tigg had rescued the little animal. The grubber had spent the first few of those days sleeping almost continuously in the little bed of grasses and rags Armindor had made for it in the wagon. From time to time it had awakened to drink thirstily and stare about with frightened but curious eyes at Tigg, Pod, and the interior of the wagon. As its periods of wakefulness grew longer and as it seemed to be responding to Armindor's spell of healing, Tigg began trying to teach it a few words. At first the boy was merely interested in passing time during the long, boring days in the bouncing wagon, but he found the little creature so intelligent and quick to learn that he had soon set to work in earnest to teach it as much as he could. As a result, it was now actually able to hold simple conversations with him.

Upon learning of Tigg's ability to communicate with the grubber, Armindor had become greatly interested in learning about it and its kind. For the past few evenings when the caravan made its nightly stop, the magician had visited Tigg's wagon, and he and the boy had spent considerable time questioning the creature.

They had learned that grubbers, like people, possessed names. This grubber's name was Reepah. And just as people called themselves humans, the grubbers had a collective name for themselves—a word that sounded like *weenitok.* The little animals lived in small tribes that were led by the oldest and most experienced member. They spent most of spring, summer, and fall gathering food—berries, fruits, nuts, seeds, and edible leaves and roots—and digging and improving their underground dwellings. During the winter months, they slept, with their communities sealed off from the outside world.

They had enemies. Reepah had received his terrible wound from an animal he called a tissik, which Armindor suspected to be a kind of wildcat. It had attacked Reepah shortly before the caravan had arrived and the soldier had discovered him. He made them understand that he had badly wounded the animal with his weapon, a sharp, pointed stick, and the tissik had dragged itself off without attempting to devour him. Another dangerous animal, he informed them, was the ruffa. These were, apparently, the wolflike wild dogs that ranged the plains in packs and had been known to attack people. And there was another enemy, the most feared of all, that grubbers called isst. Armindor could not make out what sort of creature this was when Reepah tried to describe it; it seemed to be a swift, silent, dreadfully malevolent thing that dwelt in the night and had supernatural powers. Armindor wondered if perhaps this was not the grubbers' version of what humans called dead-walkers—spirits of people who had been evil in life and returned to do evil after death.

"Soon you will be well," the magician had told Reepah just the night before. "What will you do? Will you return to the place of the weenitok?"

Tigg listened with consternation to this question. He had grown fond of the little creature and had come to regard it as a pet. He realized, however, that Armindor regarded it almost as a person and was willing to let it return to its own kind.

"Weenitok place far—far," said Reepah after some hesitation. "Reepah can't not see. Reepah not know where. Reepah live now with Minda and Tick."

Tigg had been delighted to hear this, and this morning, the last morning of their journey, he was attempting to describe their destination to the grubber.

"City," he said again. "Big. *Big*!" He stretched his arms in a wide arc. "Lots of people. Lots of houses."

"Hozzez?" questioned Reepah.

"Houses. They're like—" The boy looked about for inspiration and suddenly found it. "They're like this." He gestured at the wagon's interior. "But bigger. And they don't move like this does. They stand still, in one place."

"Uk," said the grubber. He made this sound whenever he seemed to understand what was being told to him.

"We'll be seeing the city before long," remarked Pod, who had made this journey several times. "About mid-afternoon you'll be able to make out the houses. We'll be inside the gates before sunset."

His prophecy was accurate. The sun was halfway down the sky when Tigg became aware of a grayish smudge on the horizon, which gradually resolved into walls, towers, and buildings. A feeling of excitement grew in him, and he gently picked up the grubber, cradling it in his arms, so it could see the city, too. "See, Reepah?" he asked. "*That's* a city."

"Uk," replied the grubber, peering at the view.

As the caravan drew closer to the city, it took on more of the appearance of a formal procession. The mercenaries rode in a double column ahead of the wagons, their lances unslung and held erect so that the orange and maroon pennants whipped in the breeze. When the city walls loomed no more than a mile away, a column of soldiers in black and yellow tunics came galloping out of a gate and up the road to meet the caravan. An officer conferred briefly with Pynjo and Commander Yomer, then the soldiers from the city also formed a double column and rode ahead of the others as an escort.

As the wagon containing Pod, Tigg, and Reepah rumbled beneath the high arch of the city gate, Tigg craned his neck, peering eagerly about, but he was quickly disappointed to find that Orrello seemed very much like his own city of Ingarron. The majority of the houses were constructed of logs and topped with thatched roofs, just like the common houses of Ingarron, and the public buildings and worship houses were much like those of Ingarron, too. Furthermore, the cursing cart-drivers, the vendors screeching out the merits of their wares, the brown-robed priests of Garmood clacking their prayer sticks, and all the others thronging the streets seemed identical to their counterparts in Tigg's city. But the boy detected a salty tang in the air, hinting at the nearby presence of the sea—and that was an exciting difference!

The long line of Pynjo's wagons clattered up the broad

dirt track that was Orrello's main thoroughfare, turned into a narrower side way, and passed through an open gate in a high wall, into an enormous dirt yard faced on two sides with rows of stables and with an imposing building at the far end. Tigg knew this was the city's merchant center, for it, too, was practically identical to the one in Ingarron.

Shouts from the drivers brought the plodding squnts to a halt. From the imposing building, a cluster of well-dressed figures issued forth, and with airs of self-importance made their way toward the wagons. Pynjo, dismounting, went to meet them, moving with an equal air of self-importance. On both sides of the yard, grooms, stableboys, and others whose work was the care of squnts, horses, and other beasts, called out greetings and jests as they recognized acquaintances among Pynjo's employees.

Pod tossed the reins onto the back of the nearest squnt of his wagon's team and hopped down from his perch. Cradling Reepah in his arms, Tigg followed. The grubber huddled against him as if frightened, but its bright eyes darted about with interest. Several of the stableboys caught sight of the creature and converged on Tigg.

"A grubber!" exclaimed one. "Where'd you get it?"

"You want to sell it?" inquired another. "I'll give you three whole coppers!"

Armindor appeared, laden with his bags of belongings, the two smaller of which he transferred to Tigg.

"Come," he said. "The sun will be down before long, and we must find a place to spend the night."

Calling a good-bye to Pod, Tigg followed the magician out of the great yard onto the narrow street.

"What is sell?" Reepah asked suddenly.

"Sell? Oh, uh, he wanted to give me money, and then I'd give you to him," Tigg answered. "But don't worry, Reepah, I wouldn't have done it."

"Uk," said the grubber. "What is money?"

Tigg fished inside his sash and produced an iron coin. "This is money."

The grubber studied it intently. "What is kood for?"

"Well, you see, you give some of these to someone and then they give you something you need, like food."

"What *they* do with?" persisted Reepah. "Can't not eat it!"

"Uh, they give it to someone else for something *they* need!" floundered Tigg, wondering where this would end.

There was a chuckle from Armindor. "Grubbers have a much simpler way of life than we do, Tigg. I'm afraid you'll never quite make Reepah understand how a useless bit of metal can be exchanged for something of real value such as food. I'm not at all sure *I* understand it. Ah, here is the guestinghouse that Pynjo recommended. Stay here with our things while I see about getting us a room."

They had come to a large two-story building. Above the door hung a painted sign depicting a sleeping mat, a plate of food, and a bottle. Armindor opened the door and went in.

He emerged a short time later and picked up two of the bags, leaving the two smaller ones for Tigg. "Come," he urged.

Clutching Reepah and lugging the bags, Tigg entered a large, cheerful room filled with wooden tables and benches. Thick candles in carved bone holders shed warm light that glimmered on the log walls and shone dully on the army of earthenware mugs and platters that stood in rows on shelves along one wall. The housekeeper, a burly, bushy-haired man, stood before a doorway in one corner, holding a single candle. "This way, please," he invited. "Leave your bags here; I'll send my boy up with 'em."

Tigg and Armindor followed him into a short hallway and up a flight of stairs, where he bustled along another hallway, opened a door, and ushered them into a small room containing two sleeping mats and a low wooden table with two stools beside it. There was an empty fireplace in one wall and a shuttered window in another. The housekeeper set the candle holder on the table and said, "I'll tell the boy to make a fire when he brings your things. Will you take your supper downstairs, or shall I bring it up here?"

"Bring it up, please," answered Armindor. With a bow and a quick, curious glance at the grubber in Tigg's arms, the man hurried out, closing the door behind him.

Tigg went to the window and opened the shutters. Raising himself on tiptoe, he leaned forward and put his head out the opening. Reepah clung to him and also peered out with bright-eyed interest. The window looked out upon a section of roof and a portion of the guestinghouse's yard and stables. A sea of rooftops stretched away into the distance, pierced by the occasional finger of a worship house's tower reaching toward the sky. Dusk was closing over the city, and Tigg saw no sign of what he was eagerly looking for.

"Armindor," he said plaintively, "where is the sea?"

"You wish to look upon the fabled Silver Sea, do you?" Armindor's voice rumbled behind him. "Well, you'll soon have your fill of that, my apprentice. In a day or two, we shall be sailing across it."

• • • 6 • • •

Tigg whirled, looking at the magician in surprise. Armindor was seated on one of the stools, watching him with lips quirked in a slight smile. "Did you think our journey was over? It has barely begun!"

Before Tigg could say anything, there was a thump on the door, and a bushy-haired boy about Tigg's age, wearing a stained apron over his smock and laden with their bags of belongings, struggled into the room. Depositing the bags on the floor with an audible sigh of relief, he scurried back out into the hall and reappeared moments later with a bundle of twigs, which he dumped into the fireplace. Tigg stayed silent while the boy kindled a blaze, not wishing to question Armindor in front of a stranger. As soon as the boy departed, Tigg exclaimed, "Where are we *going,* Armindor?"

"Across the Silver Sea to the city of Inbal, then north to the Land of Wemms and beyond—into the Wild Lands."

Tigg could only gape for a moment. Armindor was

calmly proposing an incredible journey, a journey which, Tigg felt sure, few people had ever made. For, from what he had heard of the Wild Lands, they made the dangerous country he had just passed through on the way here seem like a safe and pleasant park in the palace grounds of Ingarron's Lord Director. The Wild Lands were said to be a vast area thickly infested with nightmarish monsters, venomous insects, and man-eating plants, where poisonous mists drifted and the earth was racked with constant quakes! For what possible reason could the magician want to go there?

For a moment, Tigg balked at the thought of risking his skin in such a place. This was more than he had bargained for when he had made up his mind to stay with Armindor and accompany him on this journey. Again he cursed himself for not having taken the simulacrum and run away when he could.

Then he began to consider the possibilities. Think of all the strange new places and people he might see on such a journey! Think of the things he might see in the Wild Lands! A sense of adventure seized him.

Armindor, watching him with shrewd eyes, saw him suddenly grin and wriggle with excitement. The magician smiled. "Good! You've decided to see it through—again. I'm glad, Tigg. Now I can tell you more about where we're going, and why."

But at that moment there was another bump on the door, and the housekeeper entered, followed by a woman as burly and businesslike as he, the two of them bearing platters and mugs. With a flurry of motion they transferred these things to the table, bowed simultaneously like a pair of puppets at the end of a show, and left.

Orrello was, of course, a seaport, and food from the

sea was plentiful and cheap. However, such food was completely unfamiliar to an inlander like Tigg, and he scrutinized with interest the items on his platter—a large, bright blue fish with a cluster of six tentacles around its mouth, broiled on a bed of purplish seaweed; a cluster of boiled things that resembled pink caterpillars, with a bowl of spiced fish oil in which to dip them; and a pile of chunks of fried bread. Even though unfamiliar, this looked like a sumptuous feast after twenty some days of the dried meat, thin grain-gruel, and rock-hard bread that had been his fare while traveling. He plumped himself onto a stool, and he and Armindor began to sample everything. Reepah sat on the table, munching on a chunk of bread with evident contentment.

When they had finished, Armindor pushed his stool back from the table and stretched his legs, uttering a satisfied sigh. He glanced at the window, through which a portion of sky, now black and dotted with a handful of stars, could be seen. "Close that," he told Tigg, jerking his head at the window. "Voices can carry far, and what I am going to tell you, I don't want anyone else to hear."

Tigg pulled the shutters closed and hurried back to his stool.

"There was once a magician known as Karvn the Wise," Armindor began. "He died some seventy years ago, and during his life he was rated as one of the greatest magicians of our city of Ingarron. Among the spells he possessed was one known as the Spell of Visual Enlargement—which *I* now have." He fished into the bosom of his robe and brought out a thin necklace of braided leather strung about his neck. From the necklace hung a small leather pouch. Armindor carefully untied this and gently took from it an object that looked to Tigg like a thin, round piece of ice.

"Hold it carefully between your thumb and forefinger," the man directed, giving the object to Tigg. "Put it up to one eye and close the other eye. Look at this through it." On the table, in front of Tigg, he placed one of the small iron coins known as a bit.

The object felt smooth and cool to Tigg's fingers. Uncertainly, he followed Armindor's instructions. For a moment he saw only a hazy blur, then he gave an exclamation of astonishment, for the coin seemed to leap up at him, becoming many times bigger than its actual size. The features of the man's face on the coin had become incredibly sharp and distinct. Tigg could even discern places where the coin had been rubbed smooth and rounded by generations of fingers, and he could see tiny scabrous patches of rust that had appeared as nothing more than slight discolorations.

Amazed and delighted, Tigg began examining everything he could think of: the tabletop, the food remnants on his plate, the tips of his fingers. After a time, a chuckling Armindor took the transparent disk from the boy's hand and carefully restored it to the pouch.

"I see you're properly impressed," he remarked. "You should be. As far as I know, that's the only spell of its kind in existence, and it's beyond our power to duplicate it. It's made of glass, of course, but we can't make glass as clear as that!"

Tigg nodded, having often seen the brownish, murky, bubble-filled glass that graced the windows of a few public buildings and worship houses in Ingarron. "But, didn't that Karvn tell anyone how he made it?"

Armindor shook his head. "Karvn didn't create this spell, Tigg. It is from the Age of Magic, more than three thousand years ago!"

The boy's eyes widened. The Age of Magic was the

source of most of the stories, puppet plays, and live-actor dramas he had ever heard told or seen performed in Ingarron's market place by men and women who did such things for a living. It was the remote time of legend and fable when every man, woman, and child, so it was said, had been a magician, capable of such feats as flying through the air, speaking to one another across vast distances, and making visits to the sun, moon, and stars. To have actually held in his own hand a magical device from that ancient time of miracles was like a miracle itself.

"Where did Karvn get the spell?" he asked Armindor.

"Ah, that is the whole point of all this," the magician answered, eyeing him with a serious expression. "Karvn had a nephew who was a mercenary soldier, who came to his uncle's home one day crippled and half-blind from wounds he'd gotten in a far-off war. He sickened and died of those wounds, but before he died he told his uncle of a place far out in the Wild Lands that he and two of his comrades had stumbled onto while out foraging one day. It was a place filled with ancient spells and devices of magic that had been preserved for thousands of years! Karvn's nephew found this spell there and took it as a sample. He and the others planned to sell the secret of the place to some rich lord or magician, but there was a battle the next day, in which the two companions of Karvn's nephew were killed and the nephew received his terrible wounds. He was unconscious for days, and when he came to, he found he was in a wagon full of other wounded men and had been taken far from the place where he had discovered the trove of magic.

"In time, he managed to make his way home to his uncle, to whom he revealed the general location of the place. Karvn was an old man then and could not make such a long, dangerous journey, but he wrote down the location on a certain object, disguising the writing so that it would not easily be noticed. Not long after that, Karvn died, and his belongings were taken over by the Guild of Magicians, as is always done. Some moons ago, a wooden chest that had belonged to Karvn was given to me by the Guild to examine, for that is one of my duties. After some time I discovered that it contained a secret, hidden compartment. Inside that compartment was the Spell of Visual Enlargement together with a scroll Karvn had written recounting the tale I have just told you and the object that contains the location of the place of magic. So you see, I know where the place is, and I have been empowered by the Guild to go there, in secret, to secure the treasure of magic!"

"That's where we're going!" exclaimed Tigg.

Armindor smiled and opened his mouth to reply. But at that moment, Reepah, who had been curled up by Tigg's elbow on the table, half napping, suddenly shot upright and flung out both paws to point at the window. "One listens there!" he shrieked.

It took a moment for Armindor to act, but Tigg, his senses fine-tuned for instant action that had often been needed to get him out of trouble, moved immediately. He shot off the stool and was at the window in a single bound, throwing open the shutters. He saw nothing but a short expanse of the sloping thatched roof, onto which the light from the room spilled for a little distance. For just an instant he thought he heard a soft scratching sound, but then there was only the faint sigh of the night wind.

Armindor had heaved his bulk off the stool and hurried to join the boy at the window. "Did you see anyone?"

"No," said Tigg. He hesitated a moment, then said, "I'm not sure, Armindor, but I think I did *hear* something. A sort of quick scratching noise, like something on the roof."

Armindor gently moved him out of the way and pushed his own head and shoulders out of the opening. For a time he swung his head about, trying to peer through the darkness and straining his ears for a sound. Then he slowly drew back into the room, straightened up, and pulled the shutters together.

"I suppose someone could have climbed onto the roof from the courtyard," he said. "But I don't see how a man could have—"

"*Not* man!" came the grubber's shrill voice.

Tigg and Armindor turned to stare at him. He was crouched on the table, head hunched into shoulders and lips drawn back in a snarl of hatred that bared his teeth. "Not man," he said again. "Was isst! Isst!"

Armindor eyed him for several moments, a tiny frown creasing his forehead. Then the man's brow cleared, and with a barely perceptible shake of his head he turned away. It was obvious to Tigg that the magician was dismissing the entire episode as nothing but a figment of the grubber's imagination. But the boy wasn't so sure. He himself firmly believed in a host of supernatural creatures, from friendly godlike spirits to malicious, bloodsucking dead-walkers, and he saw no reason why Reepah's isst might not be lurking outside in the darkness. Before retiring to his mat later that night, he made a special prayer to Durbis-Who-Watches-Over-Thieves, requesting protection during the remaining hours of night until the sun should show itself again and drive night's evil creatures away.

• • • 7 • • •

The Silver Sea was a vast expanse of rippling, glinting blue gray that reached out to the horizon—quite satisfactorily awe-inspiring to a boy who had never seen any body of water other than the narrow, dirty brown canals that wound through parts of Ingarron. The sea was the source of a thousand and one tales and legends, of such things as sea monsters, ghost ships, islands that vanished and reappeared, and underwater kingdoms of creatures half-human and half-fish. To Tigg's disappointment, he saw none of these things during the five-day voyage on the trading vessel *Wind Witch*; nothing more than some packs of ordinary, furry, broad-winged seabats that followed the ship for long distances in order to feast on the garbage thrown overboard, and squeaked and chittered at one another as they quarreled over choice tidbits.

It was twilight when the *Wind Witch* glided into Inbal harbor and eased its way alongside a wooden pier. Men at either end of the ship tossed lines to dockworkers who quickly wound them around stubby wooden pillars, securing them with a deft hitch. The cable holding the anchor hissed through its hole in the ship's side as the big stone weight plummeted down to rest on the sea bottom. A couple of crewmen picked up a plank that had been stored out of the way and slid it out through an opening in the ship's rail until its end rested on the pier. Armindor's belongings were clustered in a pile on the deck. Tigg, with Reepah slumbering on his shoulder, picked up the two smaller bundles, Armindor took one of the larger ones, and a helpful seaman of the ship's crew shouldered the other. The boy and the two men clumped down the plank and stepped out onto the docks of the city of Inbal.

Tigg, eager to see what another new city was like, peered about, but in the slightly foggy gathering darkness Inbal was nothing but a black mass dotted with the blurry orange glows of candlelit windows. The dockworkers had vanished from sight into a nearby shack farther down the pier, and the only inhabitants of Inbal that Tigg could see were two huge rats skulking in the shadows nearby, and even as he noticed them, another truly immense rat, nearly as big as Reepah, darted down the gangplank from the ship and vanished into the darkness, passing so close to Armindor that the magician involuntarily stepped aside. Well, it was no surprise to find Inbal infested with rats; Tigg and Armindor's own city of Ingarron swarmed with the creatures, and man and boy were quite used to the sight of them.

The seaman set his burden on the pier and looked expectantly at Armindor. The magician dipped a hand into the little pouch that hung on his belt and offered an iron bit, which was accepted with a grin. "Could you direct us to the nearest good guestinghouse?" Armindor asked the man.

"Straight up that way," advised the seaman, pointing. "You'll come to a fine one in just about two hundred paces." He nodded to them and trotted back up the gangplank.

Armindor bent over, reached down, and heaved the bag onto his free shoulder, staggering slightly as he tried to equalize its weight with the one over the other shoulder. "I hope that guestinghouse is no more than the two hundred paces that fellow promised," he said. "Let's go."

With Tigg at his heels he plodded off in the direction the sailor had indicated. On Tigg's shoulder, Reepah stirred and came awake. "We in city," he observed.

"Yes, sleepy one," Tigg teased him. "You slept right through our landing. This is the city of Inbal. What do you think of it?"

The grubber peered about into the darkness, his nostrils quivering. "Like other city," he pronounced. After a moment he crouched lower, tucking his head into his shoulders. "Isst here, too," he muttered in a low voice. There was a tolerant chuckle from Armindor.

Before long they came to a building with a glowing lantern hanging beside its entrance, above which, visible in the lantern light, was a wooden signboard painted with the traditional symbols of sleeping mat, bottle, and plate, which showed that the place was a guestinghouse. Armindor pushed his way through the door, Tigg behind him, and dropped his burden to the floor with a grunt of satisfaction. They found themselves in the eating room, occupied by only a few people at this time of evening when the streets would soon become unsafe. The housekeeper, a small man made even smaller by a humpback that thrust his head and shoulders down and forward, popped out of nowhere, wiping his hands on his apron. He ran an eye over Armindor's blue sage's robe and, in a northern accent Tigg found hard to follow, chirped, "What can I do for you, Your Wisdom?"

"We shall need a room and meals for a few days," Armindor announced, looming like a giant over the man. "I'm not sure exactly how long we shall be staying—just until we can pick up a caravan heading up into Wemms."

The man raised his eyebrows and pursed his lips. "Wemms? Oh, you don't want to be going *there,* Your Wisdom. They're having a war in Wemms. It would be a risk to your life to go there now!"

"War?" growled Armindor, glaring down at the fellow.

The housekeeper bobbed his head. "Yes, Your Wisdom—a civil war. The old Lord Director of Wemms died suddenly a couple of moons back—poisoned, some say—and left only a three-year-old son to inherit the director's seat. So now a couple of young Wemms lords have raised armies and are fighting one another to see who shall become the boy's 'guardian' and run things. It's split the country up badly, too, forcing folks to take one side or the other. Brother against brother and father against son!"

Armindor sighed. "Well, we have to get through Wemms somehow, and until we can find a way we'll need food and lodging."

The housekeeper nodded and gave a shrill whistle. A pair of teenage girls in food-stained aprons appeared, scooped up Armindor's bundles, and struggled with them toward a stairway at one end of the eating room. Armindor and Tigg followed them to an upstairs room not much different from the one they had occupied in Orrello.

"What are we going to do, Armindor?" questioned Tigg when the girls had left them to themselves.

"Well, in the morning we can visit the Inbal Merchant Center and see if any caravans are still going to Wemms," the magician replied, "although I greatly fear none will be. Wars are bad for business; soldiers will loot and plunder any chance they get, and a caravan full of merchandise would be a rich prize."

"What will we do if there are no caravans? Wait?"

Armindor grimaced. "I'm a fairly wealthy man, Tigg, but I couldn't afford to keep paying for meals and lodging while we wait for the end of a war that might drag on for years. No, if there are no caravans, I'll buy a small cart and a hornbeast to pull it, which I had intended to do in Wemms anyway, and we'll just go on by ourselves as best we can."

It quickly became evident that this was what they would have to do, for at the merchant center they were told no caravans would be going to Wemms in the foreseeable future. They spent the rest of the day purchasing a small, sturdy cart and docile hornbeast, and some provisions, cooking utensils, and other necessities for a long journey. With some reluctance, Armindor also bought a serviceable crossbow.

"I never thought I would need to own one of these," he commented, looking at it with distaste, "but we may have to protect ourselves against dangerous things, especially once we get out of Wemms and into the Wild Lands."

It was late afternoon when they completed all their purchasing and returned to the guestinghouse, where the wagon and hornbeast were lodged in the stable. They had a supper in their room and were just finishing it when one of the housekeeper's girls tapped on the door. "There are two soldiers here who want to talk to you, Your Wisdom," she called.

"Soldiers?" said Armindor. "I suppose they want a spell to keep them safe in battle!" He raised his voice. "Let them in."

The girl held the door open, and a man and woman came briskly into the room. The man was tall and burly, the woman small, wiry, and tough-looking, and they both wore knee-length coats of leather covered with overlapping circles of ox horn and had small, stone-headed throwing axes hanging from holders on each hip. There were scores of companies made up of men and women like this in every city. They served as police-like peacekeepers for the city's streets, formed the army when the city went to war, acted as bodyguards for rulers and nobles, and guarded merchant caravans. They served whoever would pay them.

The man bowed and began to speak. He was a dark-eyed redhead with a bushy beard and moustache. Tigg noticed that he was missing the third finger of his right hand.

"I'm called Naro Nine-Fingers, Your Wisdom," the man introduced himself. He indicated his companion. "And this is Quick Ari. We heard that you were intending to head into Wemms, and we thought maybe you could use us as guards on the journey. Things are bad in Wemms right now. All the soldiers of the Wemms peacekeeping companies are in one or another of the armies, so there's no one to uphold the law, and gangs of robbers are roaming the countryside. The armies sweep up all the food, so folks are starving, and even those who might be honest in ordinary times mightn't be above attacking you if they thought you had something to eat. Having a couple of trained fighters with you could make a difference if you ran into trouble."

Armindor regarded him thoughtfully. "It *could* be useful to have some soldiers with us," he admitted, "but I fear I couldn't pay you enough. A couple of good soldiers can surely find better wages than I can offer."

The man scratched his beard and sighed. "I'll be honest with you, Your Wisdom—things aren't good here for soldiers right now. The company we belonged to had a contract to escort caravans to Wemms, but with no caravans going there, there's no work, so the company disbanded seven days ago. The companies with contracts for caravans going in other directions are all full, and so are the Inbal peacekeeping companies. There's no work for us here, and we're down to our last irons—a couple more days and we'd have to sell our horses. So we decided to go to Wemms and sign on with one of the armies fighting there—doesn't matter which one—and at least we'd eat fairly regular. And since you're going to Wemms, we figured we'd see if we could work our way there with you and at least have a few irons by the time we got there. We'll guard you for nothing more than our meals and a couple of irons a day for each of us." He stopped, looking at Armindor with no attempt to hide the hopeful expression on his face.

Armindor nodded. "Very well, I can afford that. We plan to start out first thing in the morning, so meet us here in the guestinghouse stable yard by sunup tomorrow."

Naro grinned and Quick Ari's face also relaxed in a

smile. The man touched his forehead in a military salute. "We'll be here, sir," he promised. He gave a quick, friendly nod to Tigg; flashed a look of curiosity at Reepah, who was crouched among the dishes on the table; and with his companion withdrew from the room, closing the door gently behind him.

"Now that was a bit of luck," commented Armindor. "If things in Wemms are as bad as they say, and I don't doubt that they are, it could indeed be useful to have that pair with us. A band of starving ruffians might well be desperate enough to try to rob a sage despite his curses, but a couple of competent-looking soldiers can generally put the fear of Garmood into even a good-sized mob." He turned his glance upon Tigg. "Now then, let's give you some more lessons in reading and number work."

• • • 8 • • •

The morning dawned gray and wet, with a misty drizzle drifting down out of the sky. Tigg was grateful that the cart Armindor had purchased had a cloth roof that would keep its occupants and their baggage fairly dry. Naro and Ari, mounted on stocky yellow horses, showed up swathed in leathern, hooded cloaks, the hems of which they used to cover the loaded, cocked crossbows they carried.

Tigg hurried to pile things into the wagon while Armindor harnessed the shaggy hornbeast, and both tasks were finished about the same time. Armindor hoisted himself up onto the leather-covered board that served as the driver's seat, where Tigg, with Reepah in place on his shoulder, joined him. The magician took up the reins and waved a hand to the soldiers, and when they urged their mounts into motion, he jerked the reins to start the hornbeast clop-clopping on its way. With the two soldiers in the lead, the little procession clattered up narrow streets between rows of tightly packed houses and soon passed through one of the city gates, just opened for the day, and moved out into the countryside beyond Inbal.

Tigg had prepared himself for another uncomfortable ride like the one from Ingarron to Orrello, but was pleasantly surprised to find that this small, light wagon traveled more smoothly than the huge, heavily weighted vehicles of the Pynjo company had. Even so, he was sure he'd be shifting his weight and stamping his feet before long. "How long will it take us to reach Wemms, Armindor?"

"A few days is all. The border isn't far from Inbal. Inbal actually used to be part of Wemms, a century or so ago. It broke loose and became a free city during a civil war that was going on then. They seem to have many civil wars in Wemms!"

"Once we're in Wemms, how long will it take to get out of it and into the Wild Lands?" wondered the boy.

"As far as the directors of Wemms have always been concerned, the Wild Lands are part of their country," Armindor told him, "so I suppose you might say we never really will 'get out' of Wemms. But I estimate it will be a good thirty days more before we reach the place where we can begin searching, Tigg."

Another question occurred to Tigg. "Do the Wild Lands just go on forever, or is there something beyond them?"

The magician chuckled. "There are mountains beyond the Wild Lands, Tigg, and beyond those mountains there are other lands and cities, although we don't know much about them."

"Do people live there—or monsters?"

There was another chuckle. "People just like us, boy, although they probably have different ways. But long ago, Tigg, during the Age of Magic, all the people and places in this part of the world—here, beyond the mountains, and everywhere—belonged to just one nation. Not the scores of little chiefdoms and directorates and free cities we now have, but one great single nation with all its parts in touch with one another!"

"But terrible things happened," interjected Tigg, nodding excitedly. He had heard of this in many a play and puppet show. "The Fire from the Sky and the Winter of Death!"

Armindor nodded. "That is what the legends tell of, but we don't really know what is meant. Did people magically hurl fire through the air at each other, or did something come down from the stars? And was the sun really blotted out for a hundred days, as legend says, so that the earth became covered with frost and all the plants withered and died?" He shrugged. "Well, whatever and however it happened, legend says that the very shapes of lands and seas were changed, and that while there were billions of people in the world before the Fire and the Winter—which I can hardly believe—there were only thousands afterward. Those few survivors were our ancestors, Tigg. Their whole way of life was gone, and they and their descendents lived like animals for hundreds of years. Only slowly did people manage to climb up to where we are today.

"And where we are today is still far, far below what they had in the Age of Magic." He turned to look fully at Tigg. "You see, most of the spells that have come down to us are not objects like that spell I showed you in Orrello, they are explanations of things—explanations that were written down long ago by magicians. But we no longer understand them. The ancients used many words we can no longer fathom. For example, there's a famous spell that says it is possible to cause heat by making *molecules* move faster, but no one now has the faintest idea what these molecules might be. Are they objects that might be carved out of wood or bone? Are they bits of some kind of metal that is all gone now? For, you know, the ancients used up most metal, and what little is left we use mainly for money." He sighed and turned his gaze back to the rump of the plodding horn-beast. "Magic is simply the knowledge that the people of the Age of Magic possessed and we do not. And that is why I am a magician—I want to regain that lost knowledge!" A rapt look came over his face. "And some of it is out there in the Wild Lands, where we are going!"

Tigg eyed him thoughtfully. Armindor's words and manner had, for the first time, given the boy a glimpse of what being a magician could mean—not just wealth and respect, but also the searching out of long-lost secrets, the discovery of new things, the possession of knowledge that few others possessed. It stirred excitement in Tigg.

After a time, he said, "Armindor, I've heard it told that the Fire from the Sky *changed* a lot of the animals that were living then, so that many animals are different now from what they were like in the Age of Magic. Is that true?"

Armindor shrugged. "That's another thing no one is really sure of. Those stories you've heard are based on old writings that tell how some animals were 'mutated' by the Fire from the Sky, and while we think the word *mutated* means 'changed,' we're not certain. Old writings speak of horses, rats, and a few other creatures still with us, but they also speak of many creatures whose names we don't recognize, such as cows and bears. On the other hand, there are no mentions of such things as horn-beasts, chiseltooths, stiltstalkers, rabbideers—or of our little grubber friend there. Are those just old animals with new names, or are they indeed new creatures that were made by the Fire from the Sky?" He shrugged again and added, "If they are new creatures, think how strange they would seem to a person of the Age of Magic, eh?"

Tigg nodded, struck by that idea. And how strange to us some of their animals might seem, he mused. An absolutely astonishing thought then came to him; if some of the animals were changed by the Fire from the Sky, perhaps *people* had been changed too! Were people different, somehow, from a boy of the Age of Magic? He looked at his hands. Did a boy of that time also have ten fingers? Would his feet, too, have had ten toes? Tigg twitched his long, pointed ears. Could a Magic Age boy do that?

Man and boy were silent, each immersed in fantastic thoughts. The drizzle continued to fall, the wagon creaked along on the wet dirt road, and out on each side of it, patiently on guard, a horse and soldier kept pace, the man and woman resembling brown wraiths in their glistening hooded cloaks. The countryside was all flat plain, much of it cultivated farmland that was broken here and there by rows of trees that had been planted close together to form a fence against the wind. From time to time the travelers passed a distant farmhouse and, once, Armindor pulled the cart over to give way to a farmer driving a squnt-drawn cart piled with the huge, leafy brown vegetables known as marsh sprouts. The man stared wonderingly at the magician and boy as he passed, no doubt, thought Tigg, speculating as to who they were and why they were heading north toward troubled Wemms.

Shortly before midday the rain stopped, although the sky stayed gray, and after a time Armindor halted the wagon. He and Tigg got down to stretch their legs. Ari and Naro came cantering in to join them, and the four shared a roadside meal of smoked fish from the Silver Sea, coarse dark bread, and beer from a big keg that had been loaded onto the wagon at the guestinghouse the night before they left. The horses and hornbeast grazed on the plentiful grass by the side of the road, and Reepah was content with a chunk of bread.

"Did you teach him to talk?" Ari asked Tigg when she heard him conversing with the grubber. "That was clever of you!" She was a plain woman, whose features were not helped, in Tigg's opinion, by the blue cheek-tattooing affected by some of the northern clans, but she had a pleasant manner, and her words made Tigg glow with pride and warm to her.

"Why do they call you Quick Ari?" he asked.

"Because I move fast in a fight," she said with a smile. She eyed him appraisingly. "Are you the sage's apprentice, or a relative, or what?"

"I'm his apprentice," said the boy with a trace of smugness.

"Ah!" She exclaimed. "Not everyone can be a sage; it takes better brains than most people have. But it's easy to see you have clever brains, and that's why the sage chose you for his apprentice."

Tigg couldn't keep from grinning proudly, but her words made him think. It was quite true that not everyone could be a sage; for while most people really just slipped into their life's work by chance, sages were *chosen*, as he had been chosen. And for the first time it occurred to Tigg that Armindor had literally chosen him in preference to anyone else in the world! It's me, Tigg, that he wants most of all, thought the boy, and suddenly realized this made him tremendously proud and happy.

The afternoon part of the journey was a repetition of the morning, except for the lack of rain. Late in the day the sun came out, just in time to set. Armindor drove the wagon off the road and stopped for the night. For the evening meal he made a small fire and fried chunks of bread in oil, to go with the smoked fish. He and Tigg went to sleep in the wagon, while Ari rolled up in her cloak on the grass and Naro hunkered down by the guttering fire to keep watch for half the night, switching places with the woman for the other half. Even though this was settled country, dotted with farms, there was nevertheless a possibility of danger from certain things that prowled in the night, on two legs as well as on four or more, and the soldiers were doing what they had been hired to do.

The next day was much the same as the first had been, but shortly after noon of the day following, the wagon rumbled past a man-high pillar of red stone, and Naro came riding up to inform them that this was a border marker of the land of Wemms.

"What do you want to do now, Your Wisdom?" he asked, cocking his head slightly and regarding Armindor. "Pay us off and go on to wherever it is in Wemms that you're going, or might you want us to stay on with you for a while yet?"

Ari cantered in from the other side and joined him, to hear Armindor's decision. The magician had halted the hornbeast and sat gazing down at them from the height of the driver's seat. "We are not going to stop in Wemms; we are heading on into the Wild Lands," he told them. "If you would like to stay with us until we reach the Wild Lands, I would be happy to keep employing you."

"Glad to stay on, sir," said the man. Ari nodded.

The wagon and its occupants, with a soldier riding out on either side, moved into the land of Wemms. Wemms did not appear to Tigg to be the least bit different from the land they had just quitted. He had thought it might somehow look different because of the war, but here, too, the road ran through flat, cultivated farmland, with the same sorts of little farmhouses squatting off in the distance. However, after a time the boy realized that these houses were abandoned. There was not a sign of a person, an animal, or a vehicle near any of them.

Then, around midafternoon, they came to a ruined village. It had been burned, and all that was left of it was a cluster of blackened husks of houses. They passed through it, and just beyond it they came to a huge old tree that had been decorated with ornaments of war—from its thick lower branches hung the bodies of half a dozen men. Their hands were tied behind them, their faces were stiffly contorted, their dead eyes stared unblinking into the bright golden light of the afternoon sun.

◆ ◆ ◆ 9 ◆ ◆ ◆

"Bad luck for this little place," murmured Armindor. "Apparently its people were for the 'wrong' side, and the 'right' side's army passed by."

Tigg nodded. He was not the least bit shocked by the sight; he had seen hanged people many times, for the execution of criminals by hanging was commonplace, and every day of his life there had usually been two or three corpses swinging from gibbets on the hanging hill just outside the city wall of Ingarron. And, although like Armindor he could sympathize with the misfortune that had wiped out the little village and probably all of its citizens, he was not shocked by that either. Cruelty, harsh punishments, injustice, and misfortune were as much a part of his world as the clouds that drifted overhead—so common as to be simply accepted and scarcely thought about.

Apparently an eddy of the civil war had swept through this area, for as the travelers continued along the road they saw many signs that told of recent warfare. The farmlands had been stripped bare of every growing thing, and every farmhouse they saw was a burnt and blackened ruin. Once, they passed a cluster of rotting bodies of horses and men off to one side of the road, silent evidence of some bloody skirmish. Late in the day they went through another tiny village; this one had not been burnt, but there were no people in it save for more corpses lying sprawled in the streets.

When they stopped for the night, Naro urged against making a fire. "It would be visible for thousands of paces, and there won't be any other lights hereabouts, you can be sure of that," he told Armindor. "Why call attention to ourselves? I know this land seems deserted, but I'll wager there are starving men creeping about in it who'd be delighted to eat *us*!"

Tigg was not at all happy to be camping in an area where so much violent death had taken place, for he felt sure there must be many troubled dead-walkers about. He had noticed that Reepah, too, seemed most disturbed, crouching in silence with head tucked into shoulders. "It's a bad place, Reepah," said the boy in a low voice.

"Uk," agreed the grubber. "Smells of blood! Smells of fear!" He looked about into the gathering twilight. "Weenitok—krubbers—live here once, not long ago. No more, now. Run away from blood and fear. Now only bad things here!"

"Are there any of your isst about, Reepah?" asked Armindor teasingly.

"Uk!" exclaimed the grubber. "Always isst!" Armindor smiled, but Reepah's words made Tigg even more uncomfortable. He was glad that while he was sleeping in the wagon this night, the two soldiers would be beneath it, one sleeping and the other keeping watch—although what they might do against wraiths, deadwalkers, and beings such as Reepah's isst, the boy wasn't sure.

Midway through the next day it seemed to Tigg that they were beginning to emerge from the war-torn land. The farmhouses he saw were all still abandoned, but there were untended crops in most fields, which hadn't been stripped bare by marauding soldiers. And eventually the travelers began to see signs of life—a buffalox standing in a pasture, a man bent over in a field, a group of figures moving among some distant farm buildings. These were cheering and welcome sights. The boy reflected on how odd it was that part of a countryside could be visited by death and destruction that left it lifeless and barren, while another part, less than a day's journey away, could still be thriving.

He soon discovered how this was possible. Out to the left of the wagon, Quick Ari suddenly pulled up her horse so abruptly that it reared, nickering in protest, and came galloping in toward them. "Cavalry patrol heading straight toward us," she yelled.

"Bad news," said Armindor. "I have the feeling that we've entered part of the country that's a stronghold for one of the armies. That's why these lands aren't ravaged—they're being protected." He chewed his lip thoughtfully for a moment, then bent his head forward and slipped off the thong holding the Spell of Visual Enlargement which he wore around his neck. "Tigg, soldiers in wartime have been known to rob even sages, but they generally pay no attention to children because children seldom have anything of value. So I think this might be safer if you're wearing it than if I am. And perhaps you had better keep some of the money, too."

Tigg slipped the thong over his head and stuffed a handful of coins into his belt pouch. Armindor's caution made Tigg see the need for caution in other areas. "Reepah," he said to the grubber, who was squatting beside him, "maybe you had better hide back in the wagon so these soldiers won't see you." It occurred to the boy that if there was a shortage of food in this land, Reepah might be regarded as something to eat!

"Uk," said the grubber, and scrambled out of sight.

Soon, the Wemms soldiers could be seen from the wagon, a round dozen of them filling the road. Their leader, identifiable by a couple of red-dyed feathers fastened to his leather helmet, flung up an arm and bawled an order that spread the other horsemen out into a loose ring that curved around the wagon, forcing Ari and Naro to move their horses close in beside it. Armindor tugged the hornbeast to a halt.

The Wemms commander urged his horse up to the wagon. "Who are you and what are you doing here?" he demanded of Armindor.

"I am Armindor the Magician, of Ingarron. This is my apprentice and these are two soldiers from Inbal I hired to guard us as we pass through your country."

"Well, you'll have to come with us," stated the soldier. "General Lord Clym will want to question you."

"Why? We have nothing to do with your politics here, and we have no part in your war." Armindor pointed out. "Let us go; there's nothing of value we can tell your general."

But the soldier would not be dissuaded. "The general will decide that himself. Come along!"

Armindor's placid expression changed to a menacing

frown. "You are interfering with a sage on sage's business," he warned.

The man flinched slightly and nervously licked his lips, but he still did not give in. "I must do my duty as I have been ordered," he insisted. "You can't hold that against me. And, anyway, if—if you do curse me, there are plenty of sages with our army who can take the curse off. Now, come!"

Armindor hissed through his teeth in exasperation, but he clicked the hornbeast to a start, and with Ari and Naro close to the wheels and the Wemms soldiers surrounding it in a loose circle, the wagon rumbled along behind the Wemms commander.

"You should have put a curse on him anyway!" growled Tigg.

The magician shook his head. "This fellow isn't frightened enough, Tigg. You see, a curse usually only works if the person being cursed fears it, and even then it takes a long time. So you use the threat of a curse to prevent someone from doing something—which didn't work this time—and you use an actual curse to punish someone who fears what you can do to them." A startled look came over his face, and he jerked his head around to look at the boy. "That reminds me—you don't have to worry about that simulacrum I made of you, Tigg. I have dismantled it."

Tigg looked at him for a few moments. "Thank you," he said. He really hadn't worried about the simulacrum since he had forgone running away with it back in Ingarron, because from that time on he had felt that Armindor would never really use it against him. But he understood that Armindor was now letting him know that there were no restraints at all on him. The choice to stay with the magician or not would be totally his. His freedom was complete.

After a time, the wagon jolted over a crest of land, and the man and boy beheld their destination, a distant village around which was encamped an army. It was a sight such as Tigg had never seen. A vast expanse of countryside was absolutely blotted out by tents, shacks, bedding, campfires, and a shifting, surging mass of people. The sound of thousands of voices reached Tigg as a murmur that swelled to a rumble as the wagon rolled nearer. Before long he found himself moving through throngs of soldiers, women, and children engaged in all the many activities of camp life: eating, drinking, sleeping, sewing, repairing weapons, talking, arguing, casting chance cubes, tending children, stirring pots over campfires. Everywhere there was clamor and motion. The cavalry patrol commander, his hand on the hornbeast's bridle, led the wagon into this, and people cursed as they moved aside to let it by.

The soldier brought the hornbeast to a halt near a large and imposing black-and-white-striped tent and dismounted from his horse. "All of you come with me," he ordered. Armindor and Tigg clambered from the wagon, and Naro and Ari got off their horses. Encircled by guards armed with short stabbing spears, the four followed their captor into the tent.

Much of the tent's interior was taken up by a massive wooden table littered with maps, leather helmets and gauntlets, drinking mugs, and plates smeared with remnants of food. Half a dozen people were seated on stools around the table, and from the rich reds and oranges of their clothing, Tigg assumed they were nobles and leaders of the army. His eyes were drawn to one of them who seemed to dominate the others: a tall, slim man of some thirty years, with a luxuriant blue black curly beard, full red lips, and startling dark blue eyes. His robe was a brilliant crimson, its sleeves and hem trimmed with orange leaves. Costly rings glinted on most of his fingers, a silver nose plug gleamed above his moustache, and copper pendants dangled from each ear lobe. Tigg was unimpressed by him, however, having grown up among the criminals of Ingarron, who—unlike the fawning priests, merchants, and some other citizens—regarded nobles with contempt and referred to them as bloodsuckers, after certain worms that dwelt in the canals and lived by attaching themselves to fish.

The noble looked up as the four prisoners were herded in. "What's this?" he barked in a voice used to giving orders.

The cavalry officer bowed from the waist. "My patrol found these four coming up the road out of the south borderland, Lord Clym," he reported. "The sage says he is a magician of Ingarron."

Lord Clym's dark blue eyes fastened upon Armindor's brown ones, seeking to dominate them and make them shift away from his gaze. "Now, what business can a magician of Ingarron have up here in a poor land torn by war and confusion?" he asked in a voice gone silky.

Tigg rejoiced to see that Armindor met the other's eyes firmly. "None, Lord," said the magician. "We are merely passing through."

The noble raised his eyebrows. "Why, then you must be going into the Wild Lands? For what reason might you be going *there*?"

"Sage's business," replied Armindor.

"Ah, sage's business!" repeated Lord Clym in a respectful manner that Tigg recognized to be mockery. "Sage's business in the Wild Lands? Bah!" His face suddenly hardened. "This is a clumsy story, my man; I should think my cousin's spies could do better! Oh, I knew he was sending spies to look over the land and judge the size and temper of my forces. Well, you shall never report back to him, I assure you!" He turned toward the cavalry officer. "Imprison them. I have no time now, but tomorrow we'll put them all under questioning and have the truth out of them. Keep them separated from one another, so that they have no chance to work out a story they can all agree on." He turned back to the others at the table in a manner indicating that he had dismissed the prisoners and the entire affair from his thoughts. Armindor, Ari, and Naro were immediately hustled out of the tent by the cavalry officer and several soldiers, and a single soldier seized Tigg's shoulder in a painful grip and thrust him after them.

• • • 10 • • •

"He wouldn't even listen to us!" Tigg exclaimed as he was pushed in among the other three prisoners. "He had his mind made up we were spies the moment he saw us!"

"Try not to worry, Tigg," said Armindor. "I'm sure that—"

"No talking!" shouted the cavalry officer. "Lord Clym said you weren't to talk to each other!"

Armindor gave him a disdainful glance, then turned back to Tigg. "As I say, don't worry," he began. But the officer thrust himself between them, his face red with anger.

"Don't talk, I tell you!" He slid a small stone-bladed dagger out of his sleeve and held it at Tigg's cheek. "If you talk any more, magician, I swear I'll cut the boy's ears off!"

Armindor glared, but fell silent. The prisoners were marched through the camp and into the village, where they were taken to a large building that looked as if it might once have been a guestinghouse. But it quickly became obvious that it was now a prison, maintained mostly to jail soldiers of Lord Clym's army who had committed theft, murder, and other crimes. Armed guards lounged in what had been the guestinghouse eating hall, and instead of a businesslike housekeeper, the place was run by a surly jailer with a patch over one eye.

"Lord Clym wants these prisoners kept apart from one another," the cavalry officer informed the jailer. "Put them in separate cells."

"I haven't got that many empty cells," the jailer objected. "I'll have to put two of 'em together."

"Put one of them in with one of the other prisoners," suggested the officer.

"That could cause trouble! Fights . . . murder!" objected the jailer.

An argument began, but the soldier holding Tigg broke in with a suggestion. "We could put this boy in the shack where we keep the horse fodder, Troop Leader. The door can be barred from the outside. He couldn't get out of there."

After a moment the officer agreed, and Tigg found himself being pulled away. "Good-bye, Armindor," he managed to yell before he was pushed out the door.

They hurried him out of the village and back into the thronged encampment. Shortly, they brought him to a barnlike wooden building with a single large door which one of the soldiers hauled open to reveal a dim interior filled with bundles of dried grass and hay.

"Inside," growled the officer.

But Tigg had never learned to accept defeat without lashing back. He felt he had a score to settle with this man who had brought misfortune on him and his companions—and had threatened to cut off his ears! He flung his arms about the man's waist. "Please, please don't put me in there," he howled tearfully. "Let me go, let me go!"

With a curse the man pried him loose and shoved him sprawling into the shack. The door slammed shut behind him, and there was the sound of a wooden bar being slid into place. Tigg grinned and fondled the money bag he had slipped out of the cavalry officer's pocket. He hadn't picked a pocket in more than two moons, but obviously he had lost none of his skill. As vengeance went it wasn't much, but at least it was something.

However, the boy's satisfaction at having gotten even with his captor quickly dissipated as he began to consider his situation. From what Lord Clym had said, Tigg knew that he and his companions faced torture on the coming day, and probably death by hanging soon after. But he was unwilling to simply give up and accept these prospects. I'll escape from here, he told himself, and then, somehow, I'll free Armindor and the two soldiers.

He looked over his prison. The sun was getting ready to set, and only a few feeble gleams of light were reaching into the shack through gaps between some of the boards that formed a wall, so the interior was in near darkness. But as his eyes adjusted, Tigg was able to make out that the shack was pretty well packed to three of its walls, ceiling high, with bundles of fodder. There was only a narrow portion of wall, containing the door, that was uncovered on one side, and only a small area of floor, three or four steps wide, to move around in.

He leaned against the door, pushing with both hands, but couldn't even cause it to creak. Well, that was to be expected; the door was stoutly made, and the bar that had been put into place across it was a thick plank. However, that could work to his advantage, for he doubted very much that with so stout a door and so small a prisoner the Wemms officer had bothered to put a guard outside. There was probably no one to keep him from breaking out if he could.

He tested the walls. The boards yielded very slightly to his pushes, but they were far too tough and well secured for him to break them. He felt that with a knife and a whole night in which to work he could probably have gouged an opening in them, and he cursed himself for not having stolen the cavalry officer's knife instead of a useless money bag.

He sat down, leaning back against yielding piles of fodder and began to consider what he might do. The darkness and the softness soon betrayed him. Without his being aware of it, Tigg's thoughts became a meaningless jumble that dissolved into a dream. His eyelids closed and he slept.

He came awake suddenly, in total darkness. It took him a moment to realize where he was. Obviously night had fallen outside. He had the feeling that something had happened to awaken him, but he couldn't imagine what it had been.

Then he became aware of a sound. It was a rapid, steady scratching noise, coming from somewhere close by. This was what had awakened him, he decided. But what was it?

He finally located it as coming from down low, on the shack's dirt floor. Or—from *underneath* the floor! A flood of horror washed over him as he realized that something was digging up through the ground toward him! A vision of a host of hideous monsters swirled through his thoughts.

Abruptly, the noise stopped. Then, in a hoarse whisper, a voice said, "Tick?"

An explosive sigh of relief and joy whooshed between the boy's lips. "Reepah!" He knelt down, bumping his head against the wall, and reached toward where he estimated the voice to have come from. His hands encountered a small furry body, half immersed in loose dirt. He realized that the grubber had dug his way under the shack's wall—no difficult job for a creature whose way of life depended largely upon digging in earth, and whose body was built for it. Tigg lifted up the little form and hugged it to him. "How did you ever find me?"

"All man-people have different smell," explained the grubber. "Reepah follow Tick smell to here."

Tigg had known that Reepah had a keen nose, but he was astounded to hear that the grubber could locate one human out of all the thousands in the encampment. "You're a wonder!" he exclaimed. "Did anyone see you? Did anyone try to catch you while you were coming here?"

"No man-people see Reepah. Reepah stay in wackon like Tick say, until dark come and all man-people sleep. Then Reepah come out, move fast, keep in darkest places. Come here, can't not ket in, so make hole under wall." He seemed to hesitate a moment, then asked, "Why Tick *stay* in here? Why not with Minda? Why we all stay in this place?"

Tigg knew that human ways were still mostly a mystery to the grubber and realized that Reepah probably couldn't conceive of one human holding another prisoner. "The people of this place are *making* us stay," he explained. "I can't get out of here, Reepah. The door is blocked on the outside so that I can't open it."

"Ket out through Reepah hole under wall," suggested the grubber. "Reepah make bick enough." He slid out of Tigg's grasp, and the rapid scratching sounds began once more. Tigg felt showers of dirt falling about his feet and realized with delight that the grubber had provided him with a way to escape!

Reepah worked for the space of about a hundred heartbeats, then Tigg heard him whisper, "Come" from the other side of the wall. The boy dropped flat, felt about until his hands encountered a sharp slope in the dirt floor, and lowered his head and shoulders into it. He squirmed forward, felt the rough edge of a board scrape over his back, and found his head and shoulders outside the shack. Another couple of squirms and his entire body was out. Reepah crouched beside him.

Tigg lifted his head slightly and gave a quick, sharp glance around. He could make out the shape of several small tents nearby and some huddled forms on the ground, which were probably sleeping people. No one had seen the escape, no one was coming to investigate. He was free!

The boy pulled himself to a squatting position and considered his next move. There was no doubt in his mind about what he had to do; he had to help Armindor and the two soldiers get out of the prison. But how?

If something could happen to upset the whole camp, something that would make the guards and jailer leave the prison to see what was going on, perhaps he could quickly sneak in and open the three cells. What was needed was a catastrophe of some sort, such as . . . a fire!

He fumbled at the folded cloth he wore as a belt. He

had always kept a number of things hidden in its folds: small coins, a piece of candle, and a flint-and-metal sparkmaker, which he now extracted. He stood up. "Wait for me a moment, Reepah."

He took two steps to the door of the shack and strained to quietly push back the plank barring it, just far enough so he could ease the door open a crack and get his head and arms inside. He snapped flint against metal and sent a cascade of bright sparks arching into the nearest bundle of dried grass. Another snap, another shower. A tiny, crawling red bug of flame appeared on the grass and began to spread swiftly.

In a moment, Tigg was back outside. He picked up Reepah and, carrying him as one might carry a pet animal, began to walk quickly but calmly in the direction of the village. The camp was full of children, and anyone who might wake up and see him would take him for a camp child, Tigg was sure, as long as he acted like a camp child. He might arouse suspicion only if he ran or sneaked, so he walked, carefully skirting each sleeping form he came to, moving softly around each tent. He had covered several hundred paces before he began to hear shouts of alarm sounding behind him. He glanced back. There were now a number of tents between him and the shack, but he could see a smudge of orange glow creeping into the sky.

By the time he reached the village, the whole encampment was awake and clamoring. He slipped among the houses, staying well in the shadows. From a nearby street came the sound of several pairs of running feet heading into the camp. He hoped it was the prison guards.

When he reached the prison building, he was delighted to see light spilling out through the main door, which was ajar, as if someone leaving in a hurry had forgotten to close it. Cautiously, Tigg peered around the edge of the door. He gave a low exclamation and jerked back.

The large room that he'd been in just that afternoon was empty save for one man: the surly faced jailer. The man was seated at a table, his body slumped forward and his head resting on the table in a pool of blood. He was clearly dead!

Tigg had no idea what might have happened, but he seized his chance. He darted into the room and glanced about, trying to find an entrance that would lead to the cells where Armindor and the soldiers were. A half-open door in the far wall caught his eye, and through it he could see the top steps of a stairway leading downward. It seemed logical that some cells might be in what was once the guestinghouse's cellar. Still cradling Reepah in his arms, he dashed to the door and scurried down the steps.

A lantern hanging from a wall peg near the bottom of the stairs showed that the cellar had indeed been altered to serve as a place of imprisonment. A narrow corridor stretched off into darkness, and on either side of it was a row of barred doors. Loud snores were coming from behind some of them.

But three of the doors stood ajar. Their bars had been slid aside.

Tigg darted to the nearest one and peered into the cell. It was empty. Reepah stirred in his arms.

"Minda's smell here," the grubber whispered. "Minda was here. He ko away."

Tigg gave a hiss of delight. Obviously the magician and the two soldiers had somehow managed to get out of their cells. One of them had probably killed the jailer. They had escaped!

The boy whirled and dashed up the stairs. The guards might return at any moment, and he certainly didn't want to be trapped in here now that everything had turned out so well. He was free, Armindor and Ari and Naro were free—he could scarcely believe how their luck had changed.

He sped through the prison door, across the street, and into thick darkness where he paused to consider what to do next. Armindor was around somewhere, probably looking for him. Tigg felt sure that Reepah's marvelous nose could lead him to the magician.

"Reepah, can you find Armindor by smell, as you found me?" he whispered.

"Uk," said the grubber. "Can find. But Minda ko back into place where all people are—place we just come from."

He means the army camp, thought Tigg, and became suddenly aware, once again, of the shouting and tumult which he had simply been ignoring in concentrating on finding Armindor. Did he dare go back into the camp among all those now wide-awake and excited people? What if someone should notice him and question him? What if the cavalry officer or one of the soldiers should see him and recognize him? To go back into the encampment was to run the risk of recapture, but there was nothing else to do if he was to rejoin his friend.

"All right, Reepah," he said. "Let's find Armindor."

• • • 11 • • •

Armindor had watched with consternation as Tigg was dragged off through the prison door. The magician had felt he could provide some protection for the boy as long as they were together, but now there was nothing he could do. He had become very fond of the skinny, dark-eyed twelve-year-old and was tormented by the thought that Tigg might be mistreated by the cavalry officer and soldiers. Cruelty to helpless prisoners was a common pastime for such men.

Tigg had become a very important part of Armindor's life, yet it had been just sheer chance and a sudden whim that had led him to "recruit" the boy as an apprentice. He had stepped out of his house that night two moons ago in Ingarron just in time to see Tigg do his whining-beggar act and pick the merchant's pocket. Armindor had felt no concern for the merchant; the man was a fool for being in the streets at night in the first place, and he'd looked as if he could easily afford the loss of his money bag. But Tigg's acting ability, his dexterity, and the air of "I can handle the whole world" that he projected had roused Armindor's admiration and interest. He had set his trap—coughing to attract the boy's attention and deliberately leaving the door ajar as he seemingly walked off to attend to some errand. He had quickly doubled back and been elated to see that Tigg had taken the bait, which indicated courage on the boy's part. And after talking with Tigg for a short time, Armindor had decided he possessed all the qualities needed to become a magician and had bound him as an apprentice, using the trick with the wax doll.

But Armindor had actually surprised himself by his sudden decision to take on an apprentice. In thinking about it, he realized that, faced with the closing years of his life—for he was an old and long-lived man in his world—he had a burning desire to pass on his knowledge and his love of magic to someone who would also love and nurture and expand it as he had. And somehow he had felt that this ignorant, ragged, gutter-bred thief would be the one.

He had watched, hopefully, and seen his belief become reality. He had rejoiced when Tigg had made the choice to stay with him. He had been gladdened to see Tigg's compassion for the wounded grubber, for that was evidence that the boy's hard life in the Ingarron underworld had not coarsened and brutalized him. And Armindor was elated to see how avidly the boy took to the magical arts of reading and working with numbers. The magician now knew that he had what he had hoped for, and he also knew that he had come to love the former waif as the grandson his poor long-dead daughter and her husband, killed by plague, had never been able to give him.

But now he had put Tigg into a situation in which he faced torture and probably death!

All this was threshing in Armindor's thoughts as he was herded down the steps with Ari and Naro, and shoved into a tiny, lightless cell. The door thumped shut and he heard the heavy bar slide into place, leaving him penned and helpless. He felt his way to a rough stone wall and, with a sigh, eased himself to a sitting position on the floor, using the wall as a backrest. How, he asked himself in desperation, can I get Tigg, myself, and the two mercenaries out of this mess? At the very least, how can I keep that arrogant snake Lord Clym from torturing or killing the boy?

He had spent many hours wrestling with this problem when he heard, to his surprise, the bar on the door being quietly slid aside. The door was cautiously opened and he saw a man's figure silhouetted against the faint light of the lantern hanging by the stairs.

"Armindor," whispered Naro. "Come!"

Bubbling with a mixture of astonishment and hope, the magician scrambled to his feet and charged out of the cell. "How in the name of all the gods, spirits, and powers did you manage this?" he whispered.

Naro gave a quick shake of his head, indicating he didn't wish to take the time to explain. "We've got to get out of here. Come on." He gripped the magician's arm.

"Ari," said Armindor, holding back. "Where's she?"

"I don't know what cell she's in," hissed the soldier impatiently. "In Great Garmood's name, sage, let's *go*!"

"Not without her," insisted Armindor. "I saw where they put her—it's this one." Hastily he shoved the thick wooden bar aside and yanked open the door. "Ari!" he whispered.

In a moment the woman came lurching out, rubbing her eyes as if she had been sleeping. "Come now!" demanded Naro in a harsh whisper.

They darted up the steps as quietly as possible. Naro, in the lead, eased open the door and cautiously peered around it. After a moment he opened the door wider and stepped past it. "Come on," he urged again, in a normal tone of voice.

Ari and Armindor followed, and both momentarily stopped short at the sight of the jailer slumped forward with his head on the table as if sleeping and about to waken at any moment. Then they saw that his single eye was wide open and staring, and they became aware of the glistening red pool beneath his face. They hurried to follow Naro, who flung open the outer door. In a moment they were outside in the night-dark street. Naro paused in indecision, turning his head as if to determine which way to go.

"You have great power, Your Wisdom," said Ari respectfully.

Armindor realized that the woman thought he had engineered their escape. "I had nothing to do with any of that," he told her. "Naro managed it, somehow."

"Naro?" she said in an unbelieving tone. "How?"

"Somebody helped us," said Naro after a moment. "I don't know who or why. My door opened and I heard a whispering voice tell me to leave at once, that everything would be all right. That's all I know." He looked around again. "I thought that whoever it was would be out here waiting for us."

"Whoever it was must have cut the jailer's throat," said Armindor, frowning.

"It wasn't cut," said Ari in a low voice. "It was ripped

out!" She was standing close to Armindor, and he felt her shiver.

"Well, we can't just stand here, we've got to get away!" urged Naro. "Maybe we can steal some horses and—" he broke off, listening. "What's that noise? What in Garmood's name is going on?" The night had suddenly been shattered by shouts and screams from the encampment around the village.

"There's a glow in the sky," said Ari. "A fire!"

"That may help us," exulted Naro. "It will draw everyone's attention. Come on, we can get to where the horses are kept and get out of here!"

"Not without Tigg," said Armindor. "We must find Tigg!"

Naro swore. "We don't know where that fodder shack they put him in is. We'll never find him. We've got to get away before someone discovers we've escaped!"

"Go ahead then," Armindor told him. "But I'm going to look for Tigg."

"I'll help you," Ari said. "No one will notice us if we go into the camp, with all that commotion going on. We'll find where they have the boy, and we'll get him out!"

"Come on," said Armindor, and he broke into a trot, Ari beside him. Naro swore again, but hurried to join them. They sped up the street, turned into another, and suddenly found themselves outside the village among dozens of other hurrying figures. No one paid the least attention to them. The whole army and all its followers had come awake and were surging toward the orange glow. Armindor and the two mercenaries were caught up in the tide and carried along until they reached the fringe of a huge milling crowd and could go no further.

"What's happened?" Ari asked another female soldier standing nearby, raising her voice over the clamor. "Do you know?"

"The shack where they keep the horse fodder's burning down," the woman replied, "and the fire's spread to nearby tents. The whole camp will go up if they don't put it out!" She paused a moment, then said, "I hear there was a prisoner in there, too—a boy, they say. He's a cinder by now!"

"Tigg!" Armindor exclaimed in a voice thick with horror. "No!" He pressed his hands to his face, and a terrible sob racked his big body.

Ari and Naro stood quietly beside him for a time. Then Naro took him by the arm. "It's too bad, Your Wisdom," the man murmured. "He seemed like a nice little fellow. But there's nothing we can do for him now. We've got to save ourselves. We've got to get away."

Uncaring, Armindor let them lead him away. They guided him carefully, for he could not see through the tears that were streaming from his eyes.

◆ ◆ ◆ 12 ◆ ◆ ◆

A thin, dark-haired boy carrying a pet in his arms wandered through the throngs of soldiers, women, and children who were trooping back to their sleeping places after the excitement of the fire that had roused General Lord Clym's entire encampment. The boy appeared to be searching for someone, and from time to time he spoke to his pet as if to comfort it. There was nothing at all unusual in such a sight, and no one paid the slightest attention to the boy, or even noticed that his pet was something other than an ordinary tame woodsdog or furry meadowhopper. Yet, Tigg still felt as if at any moment, he would hear a yell of "That boy—seize him!" But he trudged on, following Reepah's whispered commands to "go on," or "go this way," accompanied by a nudge of the nose on Tigg's right or left arm to indicate the direction to be taken.

After a time they came to the large paddock in which most of the army's mounts were kept. Normally, there were a few guards here, but all had gone off to watch the fire. Reepah now seemed to hesitate and become unsure of himself. They moved along the crude wooden fence surrounding the enclosure until they came to a gate that stood slightly ajar.

"They ko from here," said Reepah.

Tigg stopped dead. "What do you mean?" he asked, fear clutching at him.

"Minda and other one and one. They ko on four-foot runners."

Tigg understood all too well that Armindor and the two soldiers had ridden off on horses. He could scarcely believe it. Armindor had deserted him without even trying to find him! The boy felt crushed, and tears welled into his eyes.

And then his native intelligence went to work, and he understood what must have happened. Reepah's nose, following Armindor's scent, had led them to the blackened, ash-strewn remains of the building in which Tigg had been imprisoned, indicating that Armindor had gone there in search of the boy. But Tigg realized that the man would have had no way of knowing he had escaped from the building before it burned down. Armindor must think he was dead. Thus there would be no reason for the magician and the soldiers to risk recapture by staying in the camp to keep searching. They had stolen some horses and were heading toward the Wild Lands.

So Tigg was on his own, and it seemed to him that he had three choices. One, he could stay here and try to eke out a living by stealing, all the while running the risk of being seen by one of the men who knew him. That really didn't seem very promising. Two, he could set off back down the road and return to Inbal, a journey of probably six or seven days by foot, for he had no idea of how to ride a horse, even if he could steal one. In Inbal, he could easily make a living as a thief and pickpocket. That was a promising option. And three, he could set out into the Wild Lands in search of Armindor. There were serious drawbacks to that, of course. Even though Reepah could probably follow Armindor's trail, the magician and the two soldiers on horseback would always be far ahead, and Tigg and Reepah might never be able to catch up to them. Then, too, there was the very serious problem of getting through the Wild Lands alive, for the region abounded with dangers. No, of all the choices, this one certainly had the least to offer.

But the third choice was, of course, the only one that Tigg would even consider. For one thing, he realized that it meant a great deal to him to have someone to love, and risking death to find a loved one didn't seem too high a price to pay.

And for another thing, Tigg was no longer willing to regard himself as a thief and pickpocket. He was a magician's apprentice! He could read—a little—and he could work with numbers—a bit—and it was his destiny to become a learned and respected sage, to help regain the lost secrets of the Age of Magic. He was unwilling to give up that destiny for the doubtful safety of the life of a petty criminal who could easily end up as a starving beggar with both hands lopped off by the judges or as a corpse dangling from a gibbet on a hanging hill.

Having made up his mind, Tigg considered his situation. He wouldn't be alone; he would have Reepah with him, which meant a lot, for not only was it Reepah's nose that would make it possible to eventually rejoin Armindor, but the little grubber was also a good and loyal friend. But he and Reepah would need food for the journey, and Tigg also felt he should probably have a weapon.

Suddenly, the boy remembered that he had a good deal of money: the money Armindor had given him just before their capture, and the money in the money bag he had stolen from the cavalry officer. There was more than enough to buy the things that were needed.

By the time the camp was fully awake and stirring for the beginning of the day, the boy had left it well behind and, with Reepah on one shoulder, a quiver of arrows and water bottle slung over the other, a crossbow in his right hand and sack of bread in his left, was heading up the road, north into the Wild Lands.

Several hours and many miles ahead of him, Armindor, Naro, and Ari had stopped to water their horses at a little stream.

"We're well beyond pursuit now, I'd say," commented Naro. "They probably haven't even noticed that any horses are missing." He eyed Armindor. "What do you intend to do now, Your Wisdom?"

Armindor shrugged. "Go on into the Wild Lands," he said in a voice that held no emotion. "That's what I made the whole journey for." He had managed to bring his terrible grief for the loss of Tigg under control, but the pain was still there, though he did not show it.

Naro rubbed his chin, shot a glance at Ari, then looked back at the magician. "It won't be easy for one man to get along in the Wild Lands by himself," he commented. "It's a dangerous place, not only from creatures that are big enough to swallow a person whole, but also from such things as poisonous snakes and insects and patches of quicksand and the like. You really should have someone with you, Your Wisdom, in case of trouble." He rubbed his chin again. "Now, if you could see your way to upping our wages to maybe four irons a day—just to cover the extra danger we'd be exposed to—why Ari and I could help you take care of whatever business you have in the Wild Lands and help you get back out in one piece. What do you say?"

Armindor considered. The Wild Lands, as he well knew, were not really as dangerous as all the tales and legends made them out to be, but they *were* dangerous, and a lone man would run a great risk in them. Armindor was really not particularly concerned about the possibility of dying, but if he were to die alone in the Wild Lands, the secret of the ancient magical treasure might be lost forever. He still very much wanted to get the magical hoard out into the civilized world where its secrets could be unlocked and used for the betterment of people's lives, but to do that he probably would need help. He was a little reluctant to trust the two mercenaries, but there was no one else—now. "Very well," he said.

Naro grinned. "Fine!" The grin faded slightly. "Of course, we will need food and weapons. There's bound to be a few farms and maybe a village between here and the beginning of the Wild Lands, so maybe we could—uh—persuade someone to let us have what we need."

"We can buy what we need," said the magician, a trifle sharply. "The jailer took my knife, but he knew better than to rob a sage of his money bag."

Naro's grin returned to its full width. "All right, then! Let's be off."

Armindor bumped his heels against his horse's flanks,

urging it forward across the shallow stream. Naro prepared to follow, but Ari reached out and grabbed his arm. "Just a moment," she said in a low voice. "There's something funny going on, and I think we should talk about it, Nine-Fingers!"

He stared at her. "What do you mean?"

"Think about what happened back in that prison," she told him. "Someone killed that jailer and let us out of those cells. Who? Why? Why didn't they show themselves to us? Why didn't they do a clean knife-job on that jailer instead of tearing his throat out like a beast? I'd like to know the answers to those questions, Naro!"

He shrugged. "So would I! I admit, it has me baffled, too. But I don't think it has anything to do with us now, Ari. We're a long way from that prison, and we'll be a lot farther away before we finish this job."

She shook her head. "I'm not so sure we're leaving it behind. I've got a funny feeling. While we're in the Wild Lands I think we'd better keep an eye out for what might be behind us as well as what might be ahead!"

◆ ◆ ◆ 13 ◆ ◆ ◆

Tigg soon left the road, for he feared that a cavalry patrol might come along and recapture him. It was really just as easy to walk in the field, off to one side, as on the rutted dirt track, and there were numerous clumps of bushes and shrubs where he could hide if necessary.

He marched stolidly along without stop for the entire day. He had eaten nothing since noon yesterday, but he had gone without food for much longer periods many times during his life, and he was determined to travel as long as he could without stopping, for he knew that Armindor must now be far, far ahead. It was evening when he reached the stream where Armindor and the two soldiers had watered their horses that morning, and he decided to spend the night on its banks so as to have plenty of water for supper and breakfast. For supper, he and Reepah shared a loaf of bread and drank their fill. Then Tigg, worn out by twelve straight hours of walking, stretched out and fell fast asleep before the sun had even set.

He was awakened by the brightness of dawn shining upon his eyelids. He and Reepah breakfasted on a quarter of a loaf each and again drank as much as they could hold. Then Tigg filled the water bottle, and they started off again, the boy wading across the knee-deep stream with the grubber on his shoulder. Again they marched without stop for the whole day.

Tigg quickly realized how very lucky he was to have the grubber with him, for the countryside was Reepah's natural home and the little creature was an invaluable source of information about it. One morning as Tigg began to divide a loaf of bread, Reepah stopped him. "Plenty other things for eat here," he announced. "Come." He led the boy a few hundred steps to a sprawling thicket of raspberry bushes laden with fruit, and together they feasted. As they marched along each day the grubber gathered mushrooms whenever he saw them, dropping them into Tigg's sack, and by evening there were always more than enough for supper. Tigg had never even tasted cooked mushrooms, but he found the raw ones to be delightful.

By the eighth day Tigg noted that their surroundings had begun to change. There were no more farmhouses now, and the open fields were giving way to many thick stands of trees. The boy decided it would be safe to return to the road and found it had become narrower and more overgrown with patches of grass and plants, making it hard to see. He presumed that he and Reepah were either nearing or had reached the Wild Lands, and a little finger of fear tweaked at his stomach. But he glanced at the crossbow to make sure it was cocked, and strode on.

On the morning of the tenth day Tigg startled, and

was startled by, a little herd of rabbideers. They came suddenly bounding out of a patch of woods straight at the boy, caught sight of him, and instantly changed direction, bouncing off into the distance like rubber balls thrown against a wall. They were grayish brown furred creatures, about half as big as horses, with bushy tails, long legs, long ears, and short pear-shaped heads.

Around noon Reepah suddenly jerked upright on Tigg's shoulder, then whispered, "Lie down in bushes! Hide! Quick!" Tigg made a dive for the nearest clump of bushes. He lay flat among the bushes, peering out through a tiny opening in the leaves, his heart pounding in fear.

Something enormous, black, and shaggy came lumbering out from among the trees a few hundred paces ahead. It moved with a steady, ponderous gait that Tigg would have sworn made the ground shake, and the boy saw with horror that it was coming straight toward his hiding place. But halfway there it abruptly stopped, dropped its massive head close to earth, and made a loud snuffling noise. Then it turned at a right angle and followed off out of sight whatever scent it had found.

Tigg lay quietly for several minutes after the thing was gone. He realized that the wind was blowing toward him and Reepah, and that if it had been blowing from their direction the creature would almost certainly have smelled them and kept on coming. The boy glanced at his crossbow and thought that an arrow would have caused no more difficulty for that gigantic beast than a mosquito bite would cause him.

"What was it?" he asked in a whisper.

"Not know," answered Reepah. "Never see such before! But—smell of danger for us. Eater of flesh, blood!"

Tigg rose, a bit shakily, to his feet. They pushed on,

through land that was taking on, more and more, the appearance of a forest. The road became a narrow, scarcely visible trail that wound through endless trees. Tigg saw that it would be easy for some dangerous animal to ambush them, or for them to simply walk right into something such as that shaggy black enormity. The easygoing confidence of the first days of the journey had been driven away, and Tigg accepted the fact that he would be in constant danger from now on.

When it was late in the day and shadows began reaching out from beneath the trees, the boy began to wonder about the safety of sleeping on the ground as they had been doing in less dangerous country. Wouldn't it be better to spend the night in a tree? He expressed this idea to Reepah, but the grubber was a believer in underground tunnels, not limbs and branches. "What if fall?" he objected.

"I don't think we'd fall if we found a tree with a lot of close, twisted branches," Tigg suggested, and began to search for such a one. He finally found an ancient gray-barked oak with a tangle of thick branches that provided a reasonably safe and comfortable resting place well above the ground.

Night came on. Among the trees there were glints and glimmers and sparkles as fireflies turned on their lights and began to signal to one another. The shadows on the forest floor thickened and darkened, climbing up the tree trunks and enshrouding branches until the forest lay blanketed in blackness. But now it began to come alive with noises, some of which Tigg found worrisome. "Can you smell all these creatures that are around us in the forest?" he whispered to Reepah, who was curled up on his chest.

"Some," said the grubber.

"Would they eat us?"

"Some. Not all."

Well, that was a little comfort. "Can you still smell Armindor in all these other smells?"

"Not where is now, too far. But can smell smells left on dirt trail. Minda, one and one and four-foot runners. And isst," he added darkly.

It took a moment or two for the significance of the grubber's last word to sink in, then Tigg lifted his head in surprise. "Isst? What do you mean?"

"Isst follows after Minda," said Reepah in a low voice. Then he launched into an astounding revelation. "Reepah try tell Tick, Minda. Isst follow from when we in first city, by bick water. Come with us across bick water. Follow to place where Tick make bick fire. Was isst kill man in place where Tick look for Minda! Reepah think isst let Minda and one and one out of little rooms there—smell of isst strong by little rooms. Now, isst follow Minda and one and one."

Thunderstruck, Tigg considered the significance of all this. Unlike Armindor, who had decided that Reepah's isst was merely a figment of grubber superstition, Tigg had never doubted that they were some kind of dead-walker or monster that grubbers were able to detect. After the night in Orrello when Reepah had insisted an isst was listening outside the guestinghouse room's window, Tigg had tried to find out more about the creatures. But Reepah did not have enough human words to be able to make the boy understand fully. Tigg had gathered only that the isst were active at night, never by day; that they were sometimes seen by grubbers as dark shapes with red eyes; and that they smelled bad—but by "bad," Tigg got the impression that Reepah actually meant "evil," and it was clear he regarded the isst with hatred and loathing. Tigg had actually forgotten all about the incident in the Inbal guestinghouse and hadn't thought about these fearsome creatures of Reepah's for many days. Now, suddenly, he was confronted with the news that one or more of them had been following him, Armindor, and Reepah since Inbal; had killed the jailer in Lord Clym's prison and let Armindor and the soldiers out of their cells; and were trailing Armindor and the two through the Wild Lands!

As Tigg thought all this over, the pieces of the puzzle came together in his mind. If an isst *had* been listening at the guestinghouse window in Inbal, it had heard Armindor tell of the hoard of magical treasures. If isst had been following Armindor since then, and had helped him escape from the prison so that they could keep on following him, it was because they wanted him to lead them to that treasure.

Why? What *were* these creatures? What use could they have for the hoard of ancient human magic?

• • • 14 • • •

Tigg believed that Armindor and the two soldiers were many days ahead of him, but in this the boy was wrong. Tigg literally spent each day walking without stop from sunup to sundown, whereas the riders started later, quit earlier, and made frequent stops to water the horses, to stretch their legs, and to take midday meals, which Tigg did not do. And in the woods, on the narrow trail walled in by close-growing trees, the horses could not really go any faster than the walking boy. Thus when Armindor, Naro, and Ari reached the edge of the forest and emerged into the open, hilly countryside beyond, they were actually no more than two days ahead of Tigg, who was in the forest behind them.

When Armindor had discovered the instructions for reaching the ancient magical hoard, he had studied and studied them to commit them to memory. He carried them engraved in his mind and had no need to look at a map or written sheet. So when he and his two companions left the woods and entered the open country, the magician knew that he was less than three days from his goal.

Late in the afternoon the three riders came to a stream that snaked between two hills. It was bordered by cattails and bulrushes, and glinting dragonflies darted and hovered above it, patrolling their jealously guarded territories. Armindor recognized it as the first of a number of important landmarks. He pulled up his horse. "Let us stop here for the night," he told the two soldiers. "I want to talk to you." The time had come to let them know what he was here for.

They all dismounted and began brief preparations for a night encampment. Earlier, Ari had shot a large, fat chiseltooth with her crossbow, and now she began to skin it for their supper. Naro squatted beside her, piling twigs for a fire. Armindor dropped to a cross-legged seated position facing them.

He went right to the point. "Hidden here in the Wild Lands there is a great hoard of magical objects from the Age of Magic," he told them. "I have come to secure all these things and take them back out where they can be put to use." He paused, looking from one to the other. "I shall be frank. These things can be properly used only by magicians, so they would be of no value to anyone else. They could be sold to magicians, of course, and it might occur to you that they could become of great value to you if they were in your hands rather than mine. Do not make such a mistake. I shall put on them a curse so powerful that they would poison you if you tried to carry them off on your own! On the other hand, I will reward you greatly, with gold, for helping me get everything back to the city of Inbal."

"Well, speaking for myself, Your Wisdom," said Naro,

when he saw that Armindor had finished, "your offer of gold is good enough for me. It's more than I was expecting, and your magical things will be as safe with me as if they were no more than a bunch of rocks!"

"I'm satisfied, too," said Ari. She looked Armindor in the eye. "You really didn't have to worry about anything happening to you or your things, Your Wisdom."

Armindor nodded. "I truly didn't think so, Ari, but I felt it necessary to cover all possibilities." Actually, he did feel that the two were probably trustworthy—but one could never tell for sure, and his mention of the curse might have been the decisive factor in making them stay trustworthy! Armindor was grateful, as he had been a number of times in his life, that most people believed in curses. As for himself, he, like most magicians, had serious doubts about the more superstitious elements of their magic, such as curses.

By noon two days later, Armindor began to sight certain landmarks that indicated he was now drawing very near to his goal. Despite the grief that still weighed on him for Tigg, and despite the calmness of his nature, he felt excitement building within him. He might be on the verge of the greatest discovery that had been made in the three thousand years since the Age of Magic! Hundreds of spells as marvelous as the now-lost Spell of Visual Enlargement might lie hidden only a few more miles from where his horse's hoofs now picked their way over the ground. Answers to scores of questions that had perplexed generations of magicians might be waiting somewhere within range of his view.

The two soldiers followed Armindor's lead as he rode left along a high ridge topped by a pair of trees, then turned sharply right toward a distant dome-shaped hill. At the foot of this hill the magician urged his horse to the left again and moved in a straight line through a patch of land covered with grayish pebbles and chunks of stone. Although Armindor's face was impassive, his excitement was growing. He recognized this kind of stone, for he had examined bits of it before. It was not true stone; it was an artificial stonelike substance that the people of the Age of Magic had used for constructing great smooth roads, and there had been such a road here, Armindor could tell. Three millennia of rain and wind had dissolved the smooth surface into chunks and pebbles, among which a profusion of plant life had grown up, but he could still estimate the awesome width and perfect straightness of the construction. This was the last landmark, and by following it he would come to the place he sought.

In time, he saw it lying ahead: a small, oddly shaped hillock covered with grass and spotted with a number of shrubs, and with chunks of the grayish artificial stone projecting up here and there. It had once been part of a building, Armindor suspected, that had collapsed and been overgrown with grass and shrubs, and he knew from the description of Karvn's nephew that most of the building, largely undamaged, lay underground.

Reaching the hillock, Armindor brought his horse to a halt and dismounted. Ari followed suit as did Naro, carrying a cocked crossbow. The two soldiers silently trailed the magician as he walked slowly around the base of the hillock until he came to a cluster of bushes. He began to pull and tug branches aside, thrusting his body in among them. After a moment he stopped, his head and shoulders bent forward, his arms extended wide to separate two crossed branches. He was looking into an inky black opening into the side of the hill.

He stepped back, letting the branches spring together,

and turned. Naro was standing a few steps behind him with an interested expression on his face. Ari was off to one side, looking equally interested.

"Is this the place, Your Wisdom?" Naro asked.

"This is it," Armindor acknowledged, looking around anxiously. He wanted to find a dead tree or bush with stout branches he could make into torches so that he could go inside and explore.

Naro nodded. He lifted his crossbow to point at Ari and pulled the trigger. The arrow buried itself in the woman's chest. The impact made her stagger back three steps, then her legs gave way, and she collapsed to the ground. After a moment she painfully raised herself slightly on one elbow and stared with astonished eyes at Naro.

He ignored her. He dropped the bow and produced a knife, with which he gestured at Armindor. "Please don't try to charge me or do anything foolish, Your Wisdom," he said. "You're a big man, but you're old, and you wouldn't have a chance."

Shocked by the abrupt turn of events, Armindor could only gape for a moment, staring from Ari to the man. Then he gathered his wits. "So, you have decided to try to take it for yourself after all," he said bitterly.

But Naro shook his head. "Not me, Your Wisdom. It's the ones I work for that want it. They arranged our escape from that prison and have been following us ever since. They should catch up to us some time tonight. They only travel in darkness, see, so they're a day's length behind us—but they move fast!" He grinned. "Perhaps I should explain. They're not human, Your Wisdom. They're some kind of animal, but they're like that grubber your apprentice had; they can think and talk like we do. Smart! They call themselves reen. One of them has followed you since you left Orrello city, and when you reached Inbal it got in touch with me, because I've worked for them before, often. Oh, do they ever pay well—in gold!" He licked his lips, then glanced at Ari, who now lay with her face pressed against the ground, breathing shallowly with a rasping sound. "I was to make sure that nothing happened to you until you found the magic treasure, and I figured I'd need a little help, so I talked Ari into joining me. She didn't know about the reen, though, and they don't want people to know about them, so that's why I had to eliminate her. I'm sorry about that—" He sounded earnest, but then he shrugged. "Only, as I say, they pay well, and I do as I'm told." He pointed at the ground. "Sit down, Your Wisdom, and behave yourself while I make a fire. We have a long wait until the reen get here."

Armindor stared at him. And when these reen get here, he thought, I will be murdered as Ari has been!

· · · 15 · · ·

The morning after learning that Armindor was being followed by the mysterious isst, Tigg resumed his journey in an agony of worry. He was convinced that Armindor and the two soldiers were in mortal danger. For if the isst did, indeed, want the magical treasure and were following Armindor so he would lead them to it, it was clear that once they knew exactly where it was they would almost certainly kill the humans to get them out of the way!

Tigg knew he had to reach Armindor before the magician located the treasure, and the boy was frantic with worry because he believed Armindor must be many days ahead of him. He could not face the possibility that the one human being who meant something to him, the man who had become the only family he had ever known, might die because Tigg would be unable to warn him in time.

Tigg pushed himself along at an even faster pace now, refusing to let himself despair of not finding the magician before it was too late. He and Reepah no longer even took the time to have a breakfast or supper, but simply fed on the move whenever the grubber found something they could eat. Tigg would not even have a chance without Reepah, he knew; the grubber's nose had kept them out of danger several times during the passage through the forest, and it was Reepah who was keeping the two of them alive with his foraging.

They emerged from the forest and moved out into the open, hilly land. At the stream where Armindor and the mercenaries had made camp two days earlier, Tigg stopped only to refill the water bottle and kept on going well into darkness. And at about the moment that Armindor was discovering the opening into the hillock, Tigg was actually no more than some twenty miles behind him.

Save for the giant beast they had encountered a few days earlier and a few scares in the woods, Tigg and Reepah had not run into the hordes of dangerous, monstrous creatures that were supposed to dwell in the Wild Lands, and the boy was beginning to feel that the tales he had always heard about this place were largely untrue. He was glad to see that he and Reepah were moving through country that seemed completely bare of any kind of life save birds and insects—but he was suddenly startled when Reepah abruptly jerked upright on his shoulder and began to peer about, his nose twitching.

"What is it?" whispered Tigg.

"Stand still!" ordered the grubber. "Not move!"

Tigg froze, wondering what Reepah had seen or smelled. The grubber gave no explanation, but clambered swiftly down the boy's body and trotted out several paces ahead of him. Then he called out a long string of words in a squeaky, singsong language that was meaningless to Tigg.

Nothing happened for a moment, then a score of small forms rose up out of the tall grass on all sides where they had been crouched in hiding. He recognized them at once as grubbers, for they were all exact copies of Reepah. However, each of these grubbers carried what seemed to be a weapon: a kind of spear made of a straight sapling with all the bark peeled off and one end sharpened to a point. What can they want? wondered Tigg; why have they stopped us? He did not feel endangered, for he could not regard grubbers as anything other than friendly little creatures like Reepah. But there was a purposeful air about these grubbers that was faintly disturbing.

One of the creatures came cautiously to confront Reepah. It was pudgy and its fur had a silvery sheen, leading Tigg to believe that it must be elderly. He remembered Reepah telling him that the leader of a grubber community was generally the oldest. This must be a leader. It began to engage Reepah in squeaky, singsong conversation.

Tigg watched and listened, trying to judge the attitude of the creatures. Were he and Reepah prisoners? Did these grubbers intend to keep them from going any further? If so, Armindor was truly doomed! Tigg wondered if he could fight his way through all the little creatures.

Reepah turned and came scampering back to him. "These weenitok, like Reepah." he announced. "This their land. They see Reepah with Tick, want know what happens. Almost never others come through their land. Now, all at once, many others come—man-people on four-foot runners, then isst, then man-person and Reepah. They want know why."

"What did you tell them?" asked Tigg.

"I say you weenitok friend, man-people on four-foot runners friends, too. I say isst follow to see where man-people ko. Weenitok ask why. I say I not know why—you know. They want you tell them."

It took Tigg less than a moment to make up his mind. The secret of the magical treasures was of no importance if Armindor died; if Tigg told these creatures everything they wanted to know, maybe they would let him go on his way and he would still have a chance to save his friend.

"Tell them that one of the men, who is wise and good, knows of a great treasure of ancient man-magic near here. He came to get it and take it back for men. But the isst want it, too, and they are following the man to find out where the treasure is! When the man finds it, the isst will kill him and take it for themselves. I want to find the man and warn him, and keep the isst from getting the man-magic!"

Reepah stared up at him for a moment, as if wondering how best to translate all this, then turned and squeaked out a lengthy speech. The elderly grubber listened carefully, seeming to become more and more excited, and when Reepah grew silent he launched into a reply, pointing at the ground and making long sweeping motions with a handlike paw.

Reepah turned again to Tigg. He, too, was clearly quite excited. "Tick—weenitok leader say they *know* where place of old man-people magics is! They have seen magics, not know what kood for. But he say if isst want them, must not have, for isst do only bad! He say if you can warn man, stop isst, that is kood. Tick—he say there is quick way ket to old man-people's place from here. Underneath kround! Long straight tunnel! You be there by dark-time. Maybe still be time warn Minda, Tick, for isst *behind* Minda, leader say! And isst not travel until dark-time start!"

A surging flood of hope washed over the boy. If he could at least get to Armindor before the isst did, he could warn him. He and Armindor and the two soldiers could be ready if the isst tried to attack. "Where is it?" he exclaimed. "Where is the tunnel?"

The two grubbers made an exchange of singsong squeaks. "They show us," cried Reepah. "Come!"

The grubbers began streaming off through the grass, and Tigg rushed after them. He could not repress a wild, half-hysterical peal of laughter. He was going to save Armindor! He knew it!

The boy followed the bobbing figures of the little furry creatures across half a mile of plain until they swerved toward an oddly shaped hillock, at the foot of which they came to a clustered stop. Tigg beheld a roughly rectangular opening, formed of broken, grayish stone. These was no way for the boy to know that a vast military complex had stood here once, three thousand years before, and that this little hill and many of the others about him were remnants of buildings and installations. Below ground had been command posts, computer rooms, storage chambers, and other rooms, all linked by long corridors through which whirring vehicles had passed back and forth. The grubbers, creatures for whom the underground was home, had long before discovered these chambers and corridors and explored them, and although they made no use of any of them, they knew where each corridor led and what each room contained.

Tigg started to put a foot into the opening, but was stopped by a shout from Reepah. "No, no! Must have fire, for see."

The boy waited, literally hopping from foot to foot in his anxiety to be off, while a grubber removed a tiny bow, short pointed stick, and several other things from a woven bag it carried slung from one shoulder. Fitting the stick to the bow to form a fire drill, the grubber quickly went to work and soon had a blaze. Meanwhile, other grubbers had scattered out among nearby clumps of bushes and returned with numerous thick branches, the ends of which were held in the fire until they kindled into flame.

Reepah appeared by Tigg's feet and tugged at the boy's smock hem to be lifted up to his shoulder. "They ko with us," he announced. "Not like have isst come through their land! If can catch, will kill!" Tigg was overjoyed to have all the little creatures as allies, for even though they were small, they clearly felt capable of fighting the mysterious isst, and this gave the boy's hopes another boost.

The torches were burning steadily now, and a pair of torch-bearing grubbers scuttled through the entrance. Tigg followed them at once. He had a momentary glimpse of a large, roughly square room, one wall of which had collapsed into a pile of stone and dirt, then he was passing through another rectangular opening and following the torchbearers down a slanting incline that had once been smooth but was now cracked and broken. At the bottom of the incline he found himself in an area of darkness nearly as black as night, the light of the torches just barely revealing a suggestion of pale walls at some distance on either side, and a high ceiling overhead—a vast, wide corridor. The two torches began to move swiftly along its length, and Tigg hurried after them. Other torches were bobbing here and there behind him, and all around was the rustling patter of grubber feet.

The long journey through near darkness quickly took on the quality of a dream that seemed to go on and on and on. A number of times torches burned down until they were guttering and were used to light new branches, bunches of which were being carried by some of the grubbers. Several times Tigg became aware of odd drafts and patches of blacker darkness, visible only out of the corner of an eye, and presumed he was passing a branching tunnel or an entrance to a chamber. Around him washed the constant, squeaky murmur of grubber voices, speaking softly to one another. But Tigg did no talking with Reepah; his mind was filled with thoughts of Armindor, and with concern that he and the little army of grubbers would be in time to save the man.

Finally, the long march ended after what seemed like many hours. Tigg became aware that he had come into a small room that was filled with shapes. He had an impression of a great jumbled litter of indiscernible objects of all sizes—some stacked neatly together, some in a helter-skelter tangle, some littering the floor—and he realized with a thrill that this must be the hoard of magical things left over from ancient times. Then, he noticed that the torches had stopped moving.

"Why have we stopped?" he whispered to Reepah. For some reason it seemed necessary and fitting to whisper rather than speak aloud in this darkness, among the clutter of objects from the Age of Magic.

"We very near entrance to above kround," Reepah whispered back. "One, one, one weenitok ko see if safe ko out." That seemed wise, but Tigg could hardly contain himself from charging out to see if Armindor was nearby and if he was safe. Durbis, please let him be all right! he prayed silently.

A dreadfully long time passed. Then there was a sound of low squeaking voices.

"Bad!" Reepah breathed in his ear. "Tick—isst here! One man-people still alive, talk to isst. Other one and one man-people dead!" He hesitated. "They not know if live one Minda, Tick. Not know what Minda like. We ko see. Sneak up on isst and kill if can!"

A shuddering gasp escaped the boy's lips, and cold hands of fear were squeezing his stomach. Who was the person that was still alive—Armindor, or one of the soldiers? Tigg could not imagine why the isst had spared anyone, but he prayed it was the magician.

"We ko," whispered Reepah. "Slow. Quiet! When reach entrance must crawl through—bushes in way."

In the light of a single torch held by a grubber up ahead of him, Tigg saw broken stone stairs leading upward. Grimly clutching their little spears, grubbers were swarming up the steps. In a moment, Tigg was following them, crossbow clutched in his hand.

The stairs turned sharply, and the boy found himself suddenly in darkness. He moved on slowly, his bare feet silent on the stone. After a few moments he saw a partially obscured patch of luminous bluish black before him, and realized he was confronting an opening and it was night outside. He dropped to all fours and eased his way slowly between the trunks and lower branches of the shrubs that grew in front of the entrance. No sooner were his head and shoulders outside than he saw the glow of a campfire just some two dozen paces away. He stared toward it, his eyes widening in shock at what he saw.

• • • 16 • • •

Instead of obeying Naro's order to sit down, Armindor turned and moved to where Ari lay. He knelt beside her, lifted her arm, and felt for a pulse in her wrist. After a moment he leaned forward and put his ear to her lips to see if he could detect any breathing. With a deep sigh, he stood up. There was probably no way he could have helped her even if she were still alive, he reflected.

"She's gone, eh?" said Naro. "Well, I'm glad she didn't have to suffer a long time. She was a good soldier. We were in a few hard actions together."

Armindor regarded him thoughtfully, wondering what sort of man could cold-bloodedly kill another person who had been a friend. One who preferred gold to friendship, obviously. The magician stepped away from Ari's body and sank to the ground, crossing his legs. There was nothing to do but wait until Naro's reen, which Armindor now realized were Reepah's isst, arrived. He sighed again, thinking of Tigg. In a way, he was glad the boy wasn't here to have to suffer this long wait for certain death, but at the same time he wished Tigg *were* here, so he could talk to him. He missed the boy dreadfully. But that will be ended tonight, he thought.

Being careful to never turn his back on the magician, Naro began collecting brush and twigs for a campfire. "Might as well be comfortable and cozy, eh?" He grinned. Armindor said nothing. Naro tried several other conversational openings but finally gave up. The sun dropped lower in the sky. The soldier went to his horse, procured some strips of dried meat and a chunk of bread and began to eat. He did not offer anything to the magician, who continued to ignore him.

The sun slid out of sight behind the horizon, and darkness closed over the hills. After a time, despite his situation Armindor began to nod and doze. Naro kept the fire fed with twigs and brush. He seemed to grow more nervous as the night wore on.

"Why iss thiss one sstill alive?"

Armindor's head jerked up at the sound of the strange voice that had suddenly spoken. It was a squeaky voice that made him think of Reepah, but it spoke with an unpleasant hissing accent.

"I thought you might want to ask him questions about some of the things in there," said Naro. He licked his lips nervously.

Armindor peered in the direction toward which the soldier was looking and gasped at the sight of the three creatures that were standing just at the edge of the fire's glow. They were about the size of a cat, gray-furred, and they stood upright on two legs. A long, pinkish, whiplike tail twitched behind each of them. Their front paws were like tiny human hands, their heads bulged with the indication of a large brain, and they had distinct jaws, but there was enough left of their general features for Armindor to be able to easily tell what kind of creatures their ancestors had been. Rats—the reens' ancestors had been rats that must have been changed by the Fire from the Sky, he decided. Suddenly, he thought of the shape that had darted ashore when the *Wind Witch* had docked at Inbal. Yes, one of these things could easily have hidden on the ship, followed Tigg and him through the darkened streets of Inbal, and lurked in the shadows of Lord Clym's encampment. Their hands appeared skillful enough to be able to slide back the bar of a cell door, and their teeth were sharp enough to tear out the throat of a slumbering jailer! That they were not simply animals was made clear by the fact that all three had pouches of some kind of leather slung from thongs around their necks and two of them carried long tubes, the purpose of which was not obvious, but which were definitely artificial constructions.

The creature not carrying such a tube seemed to be the leader. It was apparently considering Naro's words. It glanced toward the hillock, a black mass in the darkness. "You are sure thiss iss it?"

"That's what he says," Naro acknowledged. "The things you want are down inside, I guess."

The creature twitched its long pointed nose in a way that made Armindor think of a nod. Then it turned its head slightly and spoke to the one nearest it. So casually that it was completely unexpected, that one lifted its tube to its mouth and swung the tube to point at Naro. There was a loud puff of breath. Naro suddenly slapped a hand to his cheek as if he had been stung by an insect, stared at the three reen with an expression of surprise, and went over backward in a sprawl of arms and legs. He did not move again.

It was the second time that day Armindor had been stunned by a murder. But after a moment he reflected that Naro had certainly received poetic justice. And now I suppose it is my turn, he thought, and prepared himself.

But the reen leader advanced a few steps, its eyes fixed on the man. They gleamed red in the firelight. "What do you know of the thingss in that place?" it hissed. Apparently it had decided to take Naro's advice and question him.

"Very little," said Armindor calmly. He did not intend to lie or try to bargain to save his life or postpone his murder. Let them kill him and have done with it. But there was something he was curious about, and he hoped he could get the creature to explain it to him. "What do you want with those things? What can *you* do with them?"

It seemed to consider for a moment whether or not to answer him. Then it said, "From those thingss we may learn the power and wissdom of long ago. We shall make the world belong to uss!" It curled back its lip in a snarl. "All other creaturess will be our sslavess—or food! All you humanss will be wiped out!"

Fury flared in Armindor. "You think you can best us?" he growled. "A handful of puny little rat-spawn against millions of humans?"

The thing made a hissing sound that had an air of amusement. "Handful? For each human there are as many reen as leavess on a tree! Little? Being little iss an advantage. We have sspied on you for yearss, and you never knew. That iss how we learned your language. We live in your citiess, and you never notice uss—but the day iss coming when 'little' reen in the citiess shall rise up and kill all the big humanss there!"

Armindor was appalled, for he saw that these things were indeed a threat! They could obviously live among humans unnoticed, spy upon humans unnoticed, steal and commit murder with ease. They possessed a deadly weapon, a blowgun that shot quick-acting poisoned darts. And they were as intelligent as humans—intelligent enough, he had no doubt, to be able to make use of any of the old magic that would aid them in their dreadful plan. He had to acknowledge that they represented a terrible danger to the human race, and it was a danger of which humans were not even the least bit aware! Only he knew, and there was no way he could give warning, for he was as good as dead.

The two reen with blowguns had stalked forward, and one now stood on each side of the leader. The leader regarded Armindor for a moment more, then spoke in its own language. The reen on its right lifted the blowgun toward Armindor. He glared at it in defiance; there was nothing else he could do.

There was a sudden wild shriek from nearby, and Armindor jerked his head around with a shout of amazement at the sound of a voice he had never thought to hear again. Something came hissing through the air, flashed as it entered the firelight, and struck the reen leader with a meaty *thunk*! The leader dropped, transfixed by an arrow that had actually been aimed at the reen with the blowgun. But the arrow served its purpose anyway; the reen that had been about to kill Armindor took its mouth off the blowgun and stared in surprise at its fallen companion. There was a sudden shrill howling, as of many high-pitched voices raised in a battle cry, and a score of small shapes erupted out of the darkness on all sides and charged in at the two startled reen. The rat creatures went down shrieking as grubber spears ripped into their bodies.

And Armindor stared through streaming eyes at the small, skinny, black-haired figure that was rushing toward him. "Tigg!" he bellowed in a voice that shook the night. "You're alive!" In moments, the magician's apprentice discovered for the first time in his life what it was like to be hugged. Bursting into tears himself, he hugged back as hard as he could.

◆ ◆ ◆ 17 ◆ ◆ ◆

With grubber help they buried Quick Ari the next morning—sadly, because she had been faithful to her trust and had been betrayed by a friend. They did not bury Naro Nine-Fingers, but simply dragged him off a good distance from their camp and left him, for that was all a traitor deserved. Nor did they bury the three reen, for Armindor wanted to show the rat creatures' bodies to the Guild of Magicians and the lords of Ingarron and other cities, so people would become aware of this enemy that intended to destroy them. They set the reen bodies to smoking over a slow fire to preserve them, and later they would wrap them like mummies in woven dried-grass blankets provided by the grubbers.

By midmorning they were free at last to claim the prize for which the whole dangerous journey had been made. They squeezed through the opening in the hillock and between the two bushes, kindled torches, and hurried eagerly down the broken stone steps to where the things of ancient magic lay heaped.

When he had been in this place the night before, Tigg had been much too worried about Armindor to give much thought to the meaning of the clutter of objects that filled it, but now, as he peered about at what was revealed in the torchlight, a feeling of excitement and awe flooded through him. He stood in the midst of things from the Age of Magic—things that had lain in the place for three thousand years or more! What ancient marvels might be lying here under his very eyes!

Armindor had squatted down and was gently sorting through the clutter with one hand, holding his torch above him with the other. "So old," he murmured. "A lot of it has simply been destroyed by time." He lifted a warped, split, discolored, rectangular object with even rows of little square studs projecting up from its flat surface, each bearing an unfathomable symbol. "What could this have been?"

He dropped it with a sigh. "We must look for things that haven't suffered much damage, and that we have some hope of figuring out. Look for things made of glass, Tigg, and of unrusted metal or that smooth, shiny material the ancients seemed so fond of. We'll take what we find out into the daylight and see what we can make of it."

As it turned out there was little enough for them to salvage, and what there was, was the result of the whims of chance. The room had once been a little gift shop for the personnel of the underground military installation, and while most of the cheap merchandise on display, as well as the racks and counters, had long since deteriorated into clumps of rusted metal and blobs of warped and filthy plastic, some odd things had survived—mainly children's toys packaged in plastic containers.

It was Tigg who found the first usable object and carried it up into the daylight to examine it more closely. It was a red tube in a discolored clear plastic bag, and at first the boy thought the bag was part of the object. When he finally realized it was a container, he couldn't figure out how to open it, and only after a long time, with great reluctance, did he try cutting it open with his knife. Eventually he was holding the tube in his hand, wondering what it was.

One end seemed to be very slightly loose, and the boy tugged at it experimentally. There was a click, and the thing suddenly grew to twice its length in his hands! Startled, he almost flung it away in fright, but then he realized that nothing magical had really happened. The device was simply formed of two tubes, one inside the other, and he had managed to slide the inner one out. He pushed it back, pulled it out again, several times. Obviously it was made to do this. Why?

He turned the thing to look at one of the ends. His heart gave a leap of excitement as he saw a gleam of glass. The entire circular end, formed by the edge of the tube, was filled with that pure, smooth glass of the ancients, like the glass in the Spell of Visual Enlargement, which he still had around his neck. Was there glass at the other end, too? He turned that end toward him and saw that it was different; it was covered with a kind of lid that curved inward and had a tiny circle at the center, but that circle looked as if it might be glass also. Thinking of how the Spell of Visual Enlargement had to be put close to one's eye, Tigg lifted the tube and peered into the small circle, closing the other eye. He gave a sudden yelp of delight, mixed with a tinge of fright. The tube was pointed toward a distant tree, several hundred paces away, but Tigg was seeing the tree within a circle of light, so close that he could make out individual leaves and the texture of the bark!

He scurried toward the entrance in the hillock. "Armindor!" he yelled. "Look what I've found!"

After a few moments the magician came pushing through the narrow aperture. "What is it?"

"Point it at the tree over there," said Tigg excitedly, handing the tube to him. "Look through the little hole—like you do with the Spell of Visual Enlargement."

Armindor followed his instructions and stood frozen in amazement. After a time he lowered the device from his eye and stared at it in awe. "A Spell of Far-seeing! What a wonder!" He lifted it again, swinging it slowly about to look at distant landmarks, at the clouds, at a furry daybat lazily winging its way overhead.

Eagerly, Tigg returned to the underground room, and as luck would have it, he found a second object within minutes and brought it forth into the daylight. It appeared to be a small round box in another of the transparent, slick bags. The boy had no hesitancy now about cutting open the bag, and shortly he held the box in his hand.

Its top was covered over with glass, and its bottom, fully visible, was marked with a strange design and a number of characters that looked as if they might almost be the letters of an unknown alphabet placed at intervals around a circle. In the very center of the circle, a shiny bright blue thing that resembled a slim, pointed knife blade jittered and jigged and swayed, like a live thing seeking its way out.

Tigg eyed the moving thing with distrust. *Could* it be alive? It looked like some kind of stone or metal, but—

He held himself perfectly still, trying to see whether the thing was moving on its own or whether it was the motion of his hands and body that made it quiver. Gradually, the thing subsided, but Tigg saw that the slightest motion on his part would set it to quivering and spinning again.

He knelt and placed the box on the ground. The blue blade quickly became motionless. Tigg gave the box a nudge, watched as the blade swung and jittered, then grew still. And the boy suddenly realized that when the blade came to a stop, its point always faced in the same direction.

He began to experiment, moving the box from place to place. No matter where he put it, the blade swung about and then came to a stop pointing in the same direction. Why should this be? It was completely free to point in any direction as far as he could see.

Armindor had noticed what he was doing and came to stand by him. "Have you found something else?" the man asked.

Tigg showed him the box and pointed out the odd behavior of the blue blade. Armindor held the box, peering down at it as he slowly pivoted in a circle. The blue blade did not pivot with him, but continued to point in the same direction no matter which way Armindor faced.

"What could it be for?" Tigg wondered.

Armindor shook his head. "I don't know—yet," he said. "But I shall, in time!"

After a while, almost reluctantly, they ceased their fascinated examinations of the tube and the round box and returned to the underground chamber. But now, the luck that had given them two quick finds deserted them, and they spent hours sorting through objects that had not been able to withstand the assault of some thirty centuries and had become mere rusted, time-pitted lumps that held no magic or meaning. Some even crumbled to powder when handled. By nightfall, the man and boy had made only a dozen more finds and had decided, ruefully, that this would be all there was. Apparently, Karvn's nephew's tale of a vast treasury of magic had been considerably exaggerated.

Aboveground once more, while having a meager supper, they examined six of the things they had found—those that seemed most understandable.

"Even though it was not quite what we thought it would be, it was worth it!" stated Armindor, picking up two of the things. "These two spells alone are worth all the expense and the discomfort and the danger of the whole journey!"

What he held was the Spell of Far-seeing and a thing that seemed to be a marvelous spell for cutting, which he had found and Tigg had accidentally discovered how to use. It was made entirely of perfectly preserved ancient metal, and it consisted of a pair of sharp little blades, each jutting out of a thick circle, joined together at their middles in some way so that the blades could be spread apart and then brought together. By sheer chance, Tigg had stuck a thumb and finger into the circles and suddenly realized how the thing was manipulated. A stalk of grass held between the blades when they were brought together was sheared cleanly in two.

"This is a great find, Tigg," said Armindor, examining the device. "For I think this is a spell that can be copied! The blades could be made of stone and the other parts of wood. Things like this would make the cutting of cloth and leather far easier for those who must do such work."

"But what about these things?" asked the boy, indicating them. "What are they for? What can we do with them?"

One of the objects was the little round box with the jiggling pointer. Another was a pair of small tapering cones with flat bottoms and rounded tops that had been together in a bag. They each had a number of little holes in the rounded end, but the holes were different; on one object they were tiny and numerous, while on the other they were larger and fewer. Both objects were white, but the one with the larger holes bore a golden symbol that looked like a coiling snake, while the other's symbol was a straight line with a half circle stuck onto its upper part. Examining one of the things, Armindor had discovered that its rounded top could be twisted until it came off, revealing that the cone was hollow and empty. Were they containers of some sort? But then, why did they have holes?

The third of the objects was a cylinder that tapered at one end to a cone with an opening at the tip. From the other end protruded a T-shaped stick which, Armindor had discovered, could be pulled out a ways, then pushed back in. When it was pushed in, air came hissing out of the tip of the cone, as if the thing made a tiny wind inside itself.

The fourth object was a flat piece of metal curved into a kind of stretched-out, open half-circle shape. The curved part was colored red, the two ends were silvery. The thing seemed totally inert and useless, but then they found it had a strange, almost frightening power. It could pull metal things, such as the cutter, to itself, and hold them! But—what good was that?

"They must have had some use," insisted Tigg.

"You can be sure they did," agreed Armindor, "and it is our task as magicians to find those uses, Tigg." He gestured with the far-seeing tube. "We might never have known the use of this spell if you had not thought of trying to look through it. And that is the magician's way—to take an unknown thing and study it, and try it out in different ways, and try to think how it might be like something you are familiar with." He smiled. "*You* discovered this spell, Tigg, which is why I am now sure that you can be a great magician." He paused for a moment, and then, with a touch of anxiety in his voice, added, "If you have decided yet whether you want to be."

"I've decided," said Tigg, and grinned at him. "I want to be!"

In the morning, they began making their preparations to leave, carefully wrapping the magical objects in strips of cloth torn from a spare saddlebag, packing them in with their now-diminished supplies. Tigg watched anxiously for Reepah, who had been staying with the grubber community. This was a moment the boy had been anticipating with some worry. What if the little grubber had decided to stay here, with his own kind? Tigg no longer thought of Reepah as a pet, but as a friend, and he knew he would miss him dreadfully.

When they were nearly finished with their preparations, Reepah appeared with several of the other grubbers. They were carrying an object which they carefully put down at Armindor's feet. It was a battered rectangular box made of one of the ancient metals, about as long as Tigg's arm and half as deep.

"Minda, these weenitok find this man-people box long ago," Reepah announced, looking up at the man. "Not know what kood for, but Minda and Tick can have, if want."

Armindor knelt to examine the box, and Tigg joined him. A lumpy strip of grayish metal ran evenly around all four sides of the box, and Armindor slid his fingers over it thoughtfully. "This is a seal, made by pouring molten metal all around the lid," he said, excitement in his voice. "It will have kept all air and dampness out of the box and preserved what is inside. The person who did this must have felt that someone such as you and I would find this box some day and wanted us to have what is in it. Tigg, this may be the most important treasure of all!

"Can you open it?" asked the boy.

Armindor shook his head, still lovingly rubbing the grayish strip. "Not here. It will take special tools, and heat. We must wait until we are home." He looked at Reepah. "Thank your friends for me, Reepah. Tell them we are very grateful for all the help and friendship they have given us. And tell them that the weenitok soon will no longer be alone in the struggle against the isst! Tigg and I will see to it that humans learn of this enemy and begin to fight it!"

Tigg waited until Reepah had relayed this message, which obviously gave the grubbers pleasure. Then he hesitantly reached out and touched Reepah, to gain his attention. "We are leaving this place today, Reepah. We are going back the way we came—back to the place we started from. Will you come with us, or—or will you stay here, now that you have found other weenitok?"

The grubber answered without hesitation. "Reepah stay with Tick and Minda! Want see new places, new things. Want help man-people fight isst!"

"By the nose of Roodemiss!" exclaimed Armindor, staring with respect at the little creature. "I never realized it until now—he's an adventurer, too, Tigg, just like you and me!"

They stowed the mysterious box into a bag and roped the three horses together with a long leathern line. Tigg, with Reepah on his shoulder, scrambled up behind Armindor on the lead horse. As Armindor urged the horse into a plodding walk, a drizzle began to fall from the dull gray sky. But the three friends were as happy as if they were drenched in sunshine.

About the Author

Author Tom McGowen says: "I wanted to show how the loss of much of our present common knowledge in scientific areas could affect a future culture. And how, in my opinion, there will always be individuals who seek knowledge, whether it be old and lost or new and undiscovered."

Mr. McGowen has written twenty-seven books for young people. He lives in Norridge, Illinois.